*THE JET CUT THROUGH
THE CLOUDS LIKE A BULLET . . .*

Suddenly, the bubble of a hot air balloon crashed
through the ceiling of the clouds up ahead, directly
on the downward path of the plane. Metrand cursed,
hands on the throttle. "Gear up! Full power!"

They were seconds away from the balloon, close
enough to see there were three people in it. The
balloon, too small to show up on the radar screen,
was now too big and too close. Le Bec felt his fingernails dig at his palms.

But Betrand forced his will on the fast-diving plane,
turning on a mid-air dime in a vertical U-turn . . .

THE CONCORDE

AIRPORT '79

A HIGH-FLYING EXPERIENCE IN TERROR

"THE CONCORDE—AIRPORT '79"
A JENNINGS LANG PRODUCTION
Screenplay by
ERIC ROTH
Story by
JENNINGS LANG
Directed by
DAVID LOWELL RICH
Produced by
JENNINGS LANG
Inspired by the movie, "AIRPORT,"
based on the novel by Arthur Hailey
A UNIVERSAL PICTURE

ALAIN DELON · SUSAN BLAKELY

ROBERT WAGNER · SYLVIA KRISTEL

Guest Stars

EDDIE ALBERT · BIBI ANDERSSON · CHARO

SYBIL DANNING · JOHN DAVIDSON

MONICA LEWIS · ANDREA MARCOVICCI

MERCEDES McCAMBRIDGE · MARTHA RAYE

AVERY SCHREIBER · CICELY TYSON

JIMMIE WALKER · DAVID WARNER

And Starring

GEORGE KENNEDY
as PATRONI

THE CONCORDE AIRPORT '79

A NOVEL BY KERRY STEWART
BASED ON A SCREENPLAY BY ERIC ROTH
FROM A STORY BY JENNINGS LANG

INSPIRED BY THE NOVEL AIRPORT BY ARTHUR HAILEY

J

A JOVE BOOK

Jove books are published by Jove Publications, Inc., 200 Madison Avenue, New York, NY 10016

I

Kleber waved.

"Hey," Palmer said. "Tell Maggie the answer to her question is three."

"What was his

1.

McKeever leaned against the newsstand counter and yawned at the headline of the *Washington Star*:

TERRORISTS STORM IRANIAN AIRPORT

AMERICAN 707 DOWNED

The only storm at Dulles International Airport seemed to be the one that was now rending the sky. McKeever looked out through the terminal window. The field was black and wet. Thunder growled angrily. A burst of lightning ripped through the air.

Turning slowly, he glanced at the door. He looked abstracted and slightly bored. He might have been waiting for a flight to be called—a flight to someplace where he didn't want to go. A beat-up briefcase stood at his feet. He was wearing a conservative gray suit and a raincoat. His hair was shaggy and red. His perpetually squinting eyes, under wiry brows, were a pale, almost opaque gray—deceptively hard, incurious eyes in a bony, ugly-attractive face. They showed no particular interest as a heavyset man in a camel's hair coat said, "Pardon me, fella. Can you tell me the time?" The man had a soft face; his hair was expensively barbered.

McKeever nodded and looked at his watch. "Nothing," he said. "Not a goddam thing." He looked up again without a trace of expression and shrugged. "Well, you know how terrorists are. All talk, no action."

The man in the camel's hair coat said, "Cute. I've got a change in schedule for you. A Concorde's arriving at three twenty-five. Don't know the gate yet. Cover it."

"Swell. What airline is it?"

"FWA. They just bought the plane. It's being delivered."

"So it's coming in empty."

"Yeah. But they'll have a lot of press people there. Runway ceremony."

"Sounds like fun," McKeever said flatly. He picked up a copy of *Time*. "Dull, duller, Dulles," he said.

Hamilton gave him a sidelong glance.

McKeever shrugged. Well, what the hell. So he'd lost twenty points with Hamilton now. Hamilton had been at Langley so long, he'd forgotten the rest of the world existed, except as it appeared on computer printouts. Hamilton had never been undercover, or under fire, or underpaid. A nice, fat, Agency cat. And Hamilton wasn't much in love with McKeever either.

"Get lost," he told McKeever. "Have lunch. You're relieved."

"Uh-huh." McKeever studied the paperback books, and picked up a copy of Herr's *Dispatches*.

Hamilton put down a quarter and picked up a copy of the *Washington Star*:

TERRORISTS STORM IRANIAN AIRPORT

AMERICAN 707 DOWNED

"One," McKeever said to the coffee shop hostess. "That one." He jerked his thumb toward a table with a view of the field, facing the door. When he was seated, he glanced out at the rain-battered runways. A police helicopter landed like a big bluebottle fly. *Yeah. That's how I'd do it,* he thought. *If I wanted to move on a major airport, I'd come from the sky, avoiding the screens, the fancy security devices, and the jerks like McKeever patrolling inside.*

Question: But are badguys as smart *as McKeever?*

Answer: See scars on McKeever's left knee.

He laughed dryly, and studied the room. The deadliest thing in the place was the food. The people in the coffee shop were only Typical Travelers: drip-dry ladies and double knit men; honeymooners, families, Packaged Singles; widows finally loose on the world, now that their husbands were dead; and tense-looking talkers with sweat on their chins—corporate wheelers, spinning their wheels.

There was no one familiar to him from the Langley files.

Nobody wielding an M-16.

The guys who'd attacked at Mehrabad Airport in Iran this morning had blasted their way in with Kalashnikov rifles and shot down the plane with a portable SAM—a ground-to-air missile, light enough to carry and shoot from the shoulder, big enough to total an incoming plane. And they'd promised "a similar action today." They'd neglected,

11

of course, to specify where, so airports everywhere, all around the world, had mustered their forces and were on the alert.

And nothing would happen, McKeever was sure. The only advantage terrorists had was the single, cutting edge of surprise. They wouldn't strike when the world was ready. They'd proceed on the "Candid Camera" theme: when you least expect it, you're elected.

Drumming the table, he looked at the menu. *Bacon and eggs: $4.95*. At a table behind him, a woman's voice blatted, "Oh God, you're so lucky to be going to Paris. Paris in the spring. I'd give my eyeteeth." McKeever laughed to himself. If the swap were only that easy, he thought, he'd be on the Rue de Varenne right now. And why, he wondered for the ninetieth time, was it so damn hard to get a transfer approved? All he wanted was to get back to Paris, back into action. His leg was fine, had been fine for a year, and the answers, if any, were waiting back there. Someplace in Europe there existed a link, a casual bond between terrorist groups, a central supplier of underground arms. Finding and, somehow, smashing that link was what every officer and operative in every agency wanted to do.

And it couldn't be done from a lousy coffee shop at Dulles Airport.

The other thing he couldn't seem to do was get food. He looked around impatiently for the waiter.

He saw Maggie Whelan as soon as she entered the room.

She was easy to see.

She came out of a phone booth, crossed to a table, and attracted every pair of eyes in the room.

She was wearing a clinging, pale yellow dress that seemed to be exactly the color of her hair. And her hair was exactly the color of wine, of caught candlelight, alchemists' dreams. To hell with it. McKeever lit a cigarette, angry that he found her so beautiful again. Not that he expected a morality play in which women who'd once slammed a door in his face were instantly stricken with warts, but it bothered him. Christ. After all this time, all she had to do was walk through a door and his pulse ran wild. Maggie Whelan. How about that? Woman reporter for "On The Spot News." He'd made a big point of not watching the show. So now he was watching her scratching her earlobe, lighting a cigarette, stirring her coffee, opening a large manila envelope, starting to look at some notes.

Let it go, he told himself. *Just let it go.*

She forced herself to read, even though her mind wasn't on it. Research material, facts she needed before she could interview—what the hell was his name? She scanned the first of a dozen pages.

> *Federation World Airlines, buying a Concorde. First American airline to own one. Plane to be delivered at Dulles today, 3:25. Runway ceremony: Eli Sande, president of FWA.*

Eli Sande. She looked at her watch: 2:38. The crew from WKVR wouldn't be here for another half-hour. There was time. *So concentrate,* she told herself. *Concentrate, Maggie.*

> *Champagne party to be held at the gate. Guests of note: Jacques Boulanger (Aerospatiale-France); Paul Metrand, Concorde captain; Paris film star Jeanne deLuc, plugging her*

She turned to the second page.

> *reconnaissance flights over North Vietnam.*

*   *   *

Maggie laughed, then quickly skimmed down the rest of the page, flipped a few pages, and let out a groan. The notes were all about a military plane——ironically, the Harrison military plane. She reached for the envelope and turned it over. Written across it, in Annabelle Whitman's spiky handwriting, was *F.Y.I.—JEFFREY MARKS.*

Maggie winced. In the week and a half that Annabelle Whitman had been the newsroom production assistant, she'd managed to screw up forty-eight things. Forty-nine, now. So Jeffrey was covering the Harrison flight test with notes about the movies of Jeanne deLuc.

Terrific.

She looked at the final page.

About the Concorde:

At least there was that.

Stirring her coffee, she turned to the window. The rain was a thundering downpour now, hurling itself at the window. Noisy, like pebbles tossed at the panes. She watched as some lightning cracked through the sky.

"Do you want an abortion?" the doctor had asked her an hour ago. Only an hour.

She'd shaken her head. "I want the baby."

"What about the father?"

"*What about* the father?"

"Are you planning to bring up the baby alone? Or are you planning—"

"To bring up the baby alone. I don't want to get married."

"I see." Dr. Rostey was filling his pipe. "You're thirty. I suppose you know what you're doing. I—" He looked troubled. "I'm glad, of course, Maggie. For the human race. You know, ever since all you intelligent women started choosing the pill and abortion, the gene pool's been taking a hell of a dive."

She'd laughed. "My child has impeccable genes. His father——or hers—is a genuine genius."

"Fine. But from what you seem to be saying, this genius father won't be around. And I tell you, in spite of the current wisdom, a kid needs a father. A close encounter with a second kind. What have you got against marriage, Maggie?"

All she'd said was, "I'm not against it. I'm just not *for* it. And it's not for me." She paused. "But I know he'll be a wonderful father." She smiled warmly. "He's a wonderful man." She didn't mention that he was already married.

"I see." Nodding, the doctor smiled. "Well, I'm still glad you're having the baby. Make an appointment to see me next month. Call me before that if anything's up. And, uh, try to stop smoking as soon as you can."

She looked at the cigarette in her hand and stubbed it out quickly. She looked at her watch. It was almost three. Outside, the rainfall had suddenly stopped, leaving the runway surfaces a glistening black. She had to get going.

She started to read.

2.

"About the Concorde," O'Neill read aloud with his touch of a brogue. "Capable of flying at twice the speed of sound. It looks like a giant prehistoric bird, gazing at the world through a couple of big blue Plexiglass eyes, its aluminum beak glinting in the sun, pointing disdainfully down at the ground."

From the pilot's seat, Metrand, with one eye closed, looked over his shoulder at the flight engineer. *"Tu veux rire,"* he said slowly.

O'Neill looked up from the shiny booklet. "What does that mean?"

"Loosely? 'No shit.' " Metrand turned back, flicking his eyes over the console. Exactly thirty-five minutes till landing.

Henri LeBec, in the copilot's seat, said, "It means, 'You're kidding.' "

O'Neill looked confused. "Hey, I'm just reading what the press kit says. You know, the thing from

F.W.A." Shrugging, he scratched his curly blond head. "What's wrong with it, anyway?"

Metrand just laughed. "Only the facts. When the bird's in the air, the 'beak' isn't down. It's up—like a needle shooting through space. And that, my friend, is the *point* of the design."

"Well, maybe he's describing the plane on the ground, or during ascent."

"Salaud," Metrand said, and lit a cigarette.

O'Neill rubbed his jaw. *Salaud* meant 'bastard,' that much he knew. In fact, the only French he knew was the bad stuff, which left him incapable of ordering a breakfast or a taxi in Paris, but perfectly equipped for a highway dispute. So who was Metrand calling a bastard? The guy who wrote the booklet? O'Neill read on, but this time silently.

Metrand had started preparations to land. He hooked on his harness, stubbed out his smoke, and studied the radar screen at his feet. The airspeed indicator registered 570 knots, a ground speed equivalent of 656 miles per hour; they'd been flying subsonic for the last twenty miles. No sonic booms could disturb any coastal fisherman in Maine, or break any crockery at Boston teas.

The radio crackled. "Concorde two-eight from Washington Center. Hold your altitude and turn to the right. Make that a heading of three-four-seven."

Metrand was already making the adjustments. "Roger, Washington. Three-four-seven at fifty thousand feet." Now they were once again heading out to sea.

O'Neill said, "There you go. They just changed their minds. They don't want the plane."

"No returns or exchanges," Metrand said, laughing.

The voice from Washington crackled again. The instructions were to circle at fifty thousand feet. This time a terse explanation came with it. A military flight test, delayed because of rain, was about to "put something nasty in the sky."

Smiling flatly, Metrand shook his head. Americans would sure as hell play around with language, almost as well as the French. "Something nasty." He laughed dryly at the phrase. Piloting Medevacs in Indochina, he'd seen about everything nasty there was, and been hit with a couple of nasty things too. So what was it this time? A "smart" missile? A laser-guided drone? Something that would neatly jam up his radar? Screw up his instruments? Blow up his plane? War machines. *Merde.* They got bigger and better, capable of blasting billions of people, killing the planet, and after they did, there'd be no place to go, because all the productive adventures of flight—the space probes, the "giant steps for mankind"—had been left by the wayside, impoverished, dead.

"I figure we'll be about ten minutes late," LeBec was saying.

Metrand just nodded; his straight black eyebrows met in a frown.

"*Aha!*" O'Neill said abruptly. "I get it. How do you say 'I get it' in French?"

"Depends how you mean it," Le Bec said flatly.

"Right." O'Neill nodded. He held up the booklet. "Like, 'I get it why Metrand's mad at this guy.'"

"Well, you could say *je pige*," Le Bec said.

"Well . . . *zhuh peezh*," O'Neill repeated. He laughed. "Have you seen this? 'About the Crew'?"

"Paul wouldn't let me. He grabbed it away."

"Well, here you go." O'Neill passed the booklet to LeBec, pointing at a picture of the young Paul Metrand. Scowling, square-jawed, black-haired, lean.

In fact, Paul Metrand, at forty-seven, didn't really look very different from that, LeBec thought, except for the look in his eyes. In the picture, he seemed to be gazing dreamily up at the sky.

Laughing, LeBec said, "You look like you're waiting for Santa Claus to come."

Metrand said, "How do you say 'Shut up'?"

"Forget about the picture," O'Neill was saying, "just go with the caption."

Metrand said, "How do you say 'Go to hell'?"

"Captain Paul Metrand," LeBec read aloud, "who wanted to be the first French astronaut—" Le Bec broke up. "Hey, Paul, is that true?"

"The bastard got me drunk. I talked."

"The first French astronaut." LeBec laughed again. LeBec was a big man with a big man's laugh, and it echoed noisily in the cockpit.

Metrand shot a disgusted look at LeBec. "Hey listen, I said that at about the same time that picture was taken. I was just out of flight school. I had a big idea—I wanted to visit all the planets up there. That picture—" Metrand shook his head. "I look like the only ten-year-old Concorde pilot in the world. Would *you* want to fly with a kid like that?"

"Why not?" Le Bec said. "I bet you were a damn good pilot back then."

"Yeah. Ducking flak at Dien Bien Phu." Metrand unbuckled his harness and stood. "As long as we're circling—" he grabbed a cup from a shelf on his left—"anybody else want another cup of coffee?"

LeBec and O'Neill were both shaking their heads. "My wife," O'Neill said, "has now got me going on a meat-free, salt-free, caffeine-free diet."

"Yes?" LeBec said. "So how do you feel?"

"Like I'd kill for a steak and some salty coffee."

"So why do you do it?"

"She says if I do it, I'll live to be a hundred."

Metrand, standing in the doorway leading to the cabin, said, "If NASA calls me, tell them I'll be back."

The passenger cabin was nearly empty. There were only seven people aboard, all of them crew. The plane was being delivered new and completely unused. He headed for the galley, and found Celeste, crisp in her uniform, pouring a Coke.

She lifted her glass. *"Mon capitaine?"*

Her tone was a little bit cooler than Alaska. He decided to ignore it. "Is there any more coffee?"

"Oui, mon capitaine." She crossed the galley and picked up a pot. She'd cut her hair since the last time they'd met, and it curled softly now, in smooth waves. She used to describe it as mink-colored hair. She had once asked him, "Do you think if I let it grow terribly long, I could cut it all off and then make myself a coat?"

He said, "I was surprised to see your name on the crew list."

"Life," she said, pouring some coffee in his cup, "is full of surprises. You still take it black?"

"Life?" he said. "Never. Sunny-side up."

She met his eye quickly, apparently deciding she didn't want to smile.

He nodded. "Black."

She turned with the pot, and put it back on the counter.

"I meant," he said, "I heard you'd retired."

"I did. For a while. Then I changed my mind."

"I'm glad you did." He smiled at her now.

Her answer was a shrug. "Is there anything else I can get for you, Captain?"

He looked at her slowly, taking her in. In a standard way, she'd never been pretty. A little too buck-toothed, a little too thin. But she'd always had charm, tremendous sparkle, incredible warmth. Undoubtedly she still had that warmth—just not for him. He shook his head slowly. "No. Nothing else." He watched as she turned and walked down the aisle.

He returned to the flight deck, entering as O'Neill said, "Roger, Washington."

"What's going down?"

"Not us. Not yet."

"Oh." Metrand now clipped on his headphones. "Still got some nasty things in the sky?"

"Guess so," Le Bec said.

Metrand put his coffee, untouched, on the shelf.

3.

"This is Jeffrey Marks from the Harrison Aircraft Test Facility." Marks looked up at the unit director, who nodded. "Yeah. The level's okay. But I hate your hair. Could you comb it or something?"

Marks squinted out through his windblown hair. He was standing, freezing, in the middle of the airfield, staring at a three-man television crew directed by the biggest turkey in the world. Henry Camino ought to be stuffed and served for Thanksgiving, Marks thought as he licked a finger and held it in the air. "There's a wind blowing, Henry. I got a lot of hair. What the hell can I do? What the hell does it matter?"

"You look like a slob."

"I look like a slob," Marks said flatly. "There's a test going up in seventeen minutes of the smartest little fighter-interceptor in the world, and all that's on your mind is that I look like a slob?"

"You look like a slob."

Marks blew a slow, expiring sigh. "Just run your goddam camera, Henry. Or you'll miss the goddam plane taking off."

Henry Camino's shoulders went up. "All right, Jeffrey. If you haven't got any self-respect . . ."

Marks just hooted.

The camera whirred.

"This is Jeffrey Marks at the Harrison Aircraft Test Facility in Arbor, Maryland. The plane you can see behind me on the launcher looks like a spooky yellow insect—a killer bee—and just like a bee, it can fly by itself. No pilot, no gunner, no bombardier. And yet it can quickly and unerringly find its target, and blast it out of the sky."

"Cut," Henry said.

"What's the matter now? You don't like my nose?"

"I don't like your mouth. I don't like this angle, is what I don't like. The scene is static. Enough. Let's move."

"Where?"

"Inside. Maybe we'll try a high-angle shot from the tower."

The crew had already started to move. Henry Camino, Marks had decided, was trying to turn every three-minute spot into a little *Citizen Kane*. Henry was hoping some Hollywood hotshot would look at the sensitive flow of his pictures and offer him a job on the forthcoming special, "Laverne and Shirley Meet Starsky and Hutch."

Sighing, Marks rolled his eyes to the sky, which was starting to turn gray. Maybe it would rain. He looked at his watch, and then back at the sky. It was 2:45. Maybe they'd have to cancel the test.

The end of a classically perfect day. First, he'd had to fight to get a crew here at all. "We won't have the air time," Reiger had barked. "I got five hundred feet on the business in Iran. An airliner flaming in glorious color and a battle with stereophonic screams. I don't want to cut a frame of that gold. Unless—" Reiger amended, cocking his head— "you come up with a crash." "I can try," Marks had muttered, grinning sardonically, but Reiger had nodded. "Okay. Take a crew."

So the crew turns out to be Camino & Co.; Camino, who only got his job on the show because his sister married a network VP. And then, as the final present for the day, Annabelle Whitman hustles him off with an envelope loaded with notes on the Concorde.

"Got some ID?"

Marks looked up at a bulky, uniformed security guard, and flashed his press card.

"What's in the envelope?"

"Atom ray gun."

"Funny," said the guard. He grabbed the envelope and opened it. "Papers. All right, wise guy." He handed it back. "Hold your ID up and stand over there."

Over there, Marks noted, was an X-ray machine and a metal detector. He stood in front of it. Something flashed. It was taking his picture. Well, he conceded, they had to do that. Harrison Aircraft worked for the Pentagon on secret projects. He turned to the guard. "Okay?" he said. "No bells or sirens."

The guard wrote a pass, and stuck it into a magnetized sheath with a pin on the back. "Wear this," he said and gestured with his thumb. "The elevator's there."

Marks went ahead as the guard said to Henry, "Got some ID?"

The elevator played misleading Muzak: "Let's Take An Old-Fashioned Walk." Marks stepped out of the elevator, smiling slightly, and hurtled into a pale-looking man.

"Forget it, forget it," the man said quickly. "Forget it," he repeated. Marks turned around. The elevator closed with the little man in it. Marks shook his head. The man reminded him of someone. Who? Oh, yeah. The White Rabbit. The one in *Alice in Wonderland.*

At the doorway leading into Mission Control, the magnetic sensors checked his ID. If Marks hadn't been cleared to get into the room, the door wouldn't open and an alarm would go off.

Nothing went off.

Marks went in.

Two floors down, the elevator opened. The man got out. He was small, thin, slightly balding; his face was pallid and mottled with sweat. He rubbed at it quickly with the back of his hand. Not that it helped. Under his neat herringbone suit, he could feel the patches of sweat on his shirt. His hands were shaking, his lips were dry, and his stomach was as tight as a boxer's fist.

He walked down the hallway, turned to the right, looked around quickly, and walked into David Harrison's office. The office was empty. He'd known it was empty. He crossed to the window and peered through the blinds. Two flights below, in front of the building, Roger Arden was pacing around: the burly, one-time Fed who worked as the chief of security.

Turning from the window, the man in the office groped in his pocket and pulled out a key—a key it had cost him two hundred dollars and endless hours of plotting to get. Quickly, quietly, he walked to the cherrywood filing cabinet and, kneeling, reached for the bottom drawer.

At first the key seemed to jam in the lock. It wouldn't turn, wouldn't budge, wouldn't even pull out. He could feel the sweat really drenching him now. If Harrison came in and found him like this —but the key finally cooperated.

The drawer was open. It contained rows of files with handprinted tabs:

PROJECT EASTER

PROJECT FORT

What he wanted was here, but where? Which file?

PROJECT LLAMA

PROJECT LYNN

Lynn was the name of Harrison's daughter. A longshot. He pulled out the file. His hand was so wet that he was leaving a fingerprint smudge on the tab. He should have worn gloves. Too late for that now.   ..

The file held blueprints, but not the ones he wanted.

PROJECT TREMENDOUS

PROJECT TRUCE

Think, he told himself. *There's not much time.* He twitched as he heard the door start to open. Slamming the drawer, he jumped to his feet.

Halpern came in, looking cool, impeccable, and mildly surprised. "You waiting for David?"

"Yes. I am."

"Well," Halpern shrugged, "I guess he's not coming here."

"Yes. Well. We have an appointment. He seems to be late."

"Isn't he always?" Halpern laughed. Squinting, he tilted his silver-haired head. "Parker?" he said. "You feeling okay?"

"I, uh . . ." Parker hesitated. He probably looked like hell. "I, uh . . . No, as a matter of fact. Feel like I'm coming down with the bug. My wife's been down with it for several—"

"Yeah. Well, I'll see you. I've got to find David."

The door clicked closed.

Parker was shaking. Again, he rubbed at the sweat on his face and knelt to his work.

PROJECT WALNUT

PROJECT WHY

Yes, he thought, that was Harrison's style, Harrison's sense of ironic humor.

He pulled out the file on PROJECT WHY.

Yes.

The blueprints.

The papers.

The works.

The biggest secret in the Harrison arsenal.

He folded the papers once. Too fat. They bulged in his pocket. He removed them, and split them into two separate piles. Still too bulky. He couldn't get out of the building like this. His briefcase, of course, would be examined at the door. And what if they discovered the papers were missing? Halpern had seen him in Harrison's office, and would report it.

Worry about that later. Get out of here. Fast. He shoved the papers through the belt of his slacks, and buttoned his jacket.

Opening the door, he surveyed the empty hall.

He was safe.

So far.

The Mission Control Room hummed, buzzed, blinked, blipped.

"T minus seven," somebody said. "How does she blow?"

"Fifteen knots."

"Gonna dump on us?"

"No. I don't think so."

"Good."

Reporters had arrived from the *Post* and the *Star*, but Marks had the only television crew.

He was talking to Anson McGuire, a skinny, sharp-eyed radar controller, when suddenly the air

27

seemed to growl. Thunder exploded like the crack of a rifle, and it started to rain. They could see it on the monitors showing the airfield, and hear it rattling against the windows.

"Yeah, she dumped on us," McGuire growled. He looked up at Marks. "We computed that storm, but not for another forty-five minutes."

"What happens now?"

"We wait, is what happens. The storm'll blow over. It won't be too long."

Hands hit switches.

The countdown stopped.

"Washington Center from Harrison Airfield. Game delayed on account of rain."

"Roger, Harrison."

Paxton came in—the head of public relations. He trotted over like an eager dog, carrying a dead smile in his mouth. He flung it at Marks. "Something I can get you? Coffee? Scotch?"

Marks thought it over. "I'd like an interview with Dr. Harrison. Or Dr. Halpern." He grinned. "Or both."

"Oh." Paxton seemed to be doubtful about it, or sorry he had asked. Probably both. He said he'd check, and walked from the room.

McGuire looked at Marks. "You ever meet Harrison?"

"No. What's he like?"

"Man, he is something."

"Yeah? Something good?"

McGuire nodded. "Something terrific. How old are you?"

"Me?" Marks said. "Twenty-four."

"No kidding? So am I. You know where David Harrison was, when *he* was twenty-four? Designing *and* testing his own planes." McGuire shook his head. "You know where I'd've been if I'd had his bread?"

28

"The beach at Ipanema."

"You got it."

"His brother was a pilot in 'Nam."

"Yeah. *He* got it. K.I.A. That's why Harrison's hot on drones. No more pilots getting wasted in the sky."

Marks shook his head. "Fat chance," he said. He glanced at the window. The sky was almost as dark as the field; the rain was still heavy and unrelenting. "Hey, Wilbur," he said. "You think it's gonna fly?"

"Baby, the rain must fall," McGuire said; he squinted at a radar screen. "And I'd say it's gonna stop in another ten minutes." He jerked his chin at the opening door. "Long enough to buy you an interview, pal."

Marks turned quickly, following McGuire's glance toward the door. Paxton was back, and with him was a man in his early forties, a Central Casting "Test Pilot" type, with even features and jet black hair. And hot blue eyes, Marks decided. Blue as heaven and hot as hell. Dr. David Harrison, the owner of the company, inventor of the drone.

Beaming, Paxton made quick introductions. Marks said, "Sir? I'd like you to talk about the drone, if you would."

"Sure, I'll be glad to. It's—"

"Sir?" Marks said. "I meant to the camera."

"Oh. Sure."

Marks looked at Henry looking at Harrison, and wondered if he'd ask him to fix up his hair—a lock of it was tumbling over his eye. Henry didn't. The shot was set up in front of a six-foot television screen that played back a shot of the rain-soaked drone. The sound level was tested, and Henry said, "Go."

"With me is Dr. David Harrison," Marks intoned officially. "The man who invented the Harrison drone."

"We call it the Dragonfly," Harrison mumbled.

"Would you say that louder, sir?"

"We call it the Dragonfly. 'Drone' is simply a general term. Like 'car,' you know. As opposed to 'Cadillac.' A drone is any kind of unmanned plane."

"And the Dragonfly, then, is the Cadillac of drones."

Harrison laughed. "Well, I didn't say that. But maybe I meant it. Actually, it's more like a James Bond car."

Marks picked it up. "You mean full of gimmicks? The James Bond gadgets that come to my mind had all kinds of weapons for attack and defense."

Harrison nodded, then said nothing. He looked distracted.

Marks cleared his throat. Harrison seemed to be an odd combination of opposing forces, beginning with the Harvard degree in physics that clashed with the rugged, movie-star face. His manner seemed to fluctuate from expansiveness to silence. Marks said, "Tell me what's unusual about it."

"Everything. The concept."

"And would you *explain* the concept?" Marks asked.

"That men are much more precious than machines. That metal is cheaper than human lives." Harrison leveled his blue eyes at Marks. "But I suppose what you're after is a technical answer. The concept is this: the Harrison Dragonfly out on that field is an unmanned attack plane. No pilot. It's guided by television cameras in its nose. An onboard computer uses what the television camera sees to navigate the flight path, find the enemy, and then attack him."

"And what's the difference between this and the earlier models of the drone, the ones that were used, I believe, in Vietnam?"

"The ones used in Vietnam were reconnaissance

planes. They had eyes, but not brains. There've been later models, but none of them as independent as this."

"Would you define 'independent'?"

"It doesn't require any man-made decisions. Earlier models worked like this: the on-board camera recorded the scene and sent back the image to a ground control center, where an operator sat watching the screen. When he saw an enemy target appear, he 'told' the drone it was an enemy target. But the drone itself didn't know what it was seeing. It couldn't tell a MIG-25 from a bird."

"But this one can?"

"Its computer can. And once it's found its target, it homes in on it, and then attacks it."

"Independently."

"Yes. That's right. In earlier models it was Mission Control that launched the attack. The Harrison Dragonfly attacks on its own."

"But what about the pilot in the enemy plane? He can see the Dragonfly—"

Harrison nodded. "Yes, but that's about all he can do. He can try all the maneuvers he likes, but once our baby's got him in sight, it's—it's almost as though his plane were a magnet. He'll draw the Dragonfly whatever he does."

Marks just whistled.

Harrison agreed. "It's pretty amazing."

"And how would you explain *how* it attacks?"

Harrison was frowning. "I, uh, seem to be wanted by, uh . . ." He was looking at the door. A black-haired man in a pinstriped suit stood there looking like Dick Tracy. "You'll have to excuse me," Harrison said. He went up to the man, who muttered in his ear.

Henry said, "Cut."

Paxton rushed up with his PR smile, patronizing and rubbery. "Did you get what you wanted?"

"Most of it. Thanks."

A voice said, "Here we go. T minus seven."

Marks looked out through the window again. The rain, as McGuire had predicted, had stopped.

"Anyone else you'd like to talk to?"

Another group of men had entered the room. Including the White Rabbit.

Marks asked Paxton, "Who are those guys?"

"Oh," Paxton said. "That's, uh, Morton Laver. He's an engineer. And those are Richard Topper and Carl Parker of our sales department. Would you like to meet them?"

"No," Marks said, and looked around the room for someone he *would* like to meet.

"Who's the guy talking to Harrison now?"

"That?" Paxton laughed. "That's Roger Arden. Mr. Arden's the head of our security force."

Marks nodded. So the Dick Tracy character was really what he looked like: a detective. Whether or not he'd be interesting to talk to was beside the point. He and Harrison were leaving the room.

"T minus three," a technician announced, and Marks wondered what kind of Dick Tracy business had Harrison leaving at T minus three.

Marks looked around.

Henry was busy making arty little shots of blinking computers. Approaching him, Marks said, "Okay, Henry, stop fooling around. The target plane's just about to head for the sky."

"The drone?" Henry said.

"Uh-uh. The target the drone's gonna chase. An unmanned target plane."

"Oh. Where is it?"

"On the monitor, Henry. Right on the screen." Marks pointed up at the giant video display.

"Shouldn't we be down there, shooting on the field?"

"Sure we should, Henry. But we can't get permission, so we're shooting the monitors."

"Oh."

"Jesus Christ," Marks breathed disgustedly.

"Target plane ignition," somebody said. And everyone now moved over to the windows or stared at the screen as the fighter was launched, zoomed into the sky, and headed for the ocean. Henry got the shot.

Marks took the mike. "A radio-controlled, unmanned target plane is being sent over the Atlantic Ocean. In a moment, the drone—the Harrison Dragonfly—will follow it . . ."

"Seven seconds to ignition . . . six . . . five . . ."

"Traveling at over twice the speed of sound, it can catch almost any other plane in the sky."

"One . . . Ignition."

The Dragonfly blasted from its launching cradle, and shot through the sky. Banking, it turned, heading for the ocean, following the fighter.

Monitors showed the Dragonfly's view. Clouds, as the Dragonfly pushed its way through them, then the fighter.

"In range, in range," a technician's voice said. "The target's in range."

Another said, "Target avoidance procedure."

The target plane rolled and then banked steeply, trying to shake off the oncoming drone.

But the Dragonfly banked, rolled, and dove, mimicking the evasive action.

"No way the target can avoid attack," Marks said urgently. "Repeat: no way."

Again, the target maneuvered and climbed. The Dragonfly followed.

"The attack, when it comes, won't be with guns or even a missile. The Dragonfly is a suicide plane, a Kamikaze without a pilot. And here she goes."

The Dragonfly narrowed its distance from the

fighter and dove straight at it, hitting it broadside. The monitors cannected to the Dragonfly's on-board cameras went black, while the surface-based tracking cameras recorded a brilliant burst of flame.

"Dragonfly testing will continue tomorrow. This is Jeffrey Marks for "On The Spot News.' "

A cheer went up in Mission Control.

A man moved quickly away from the envelope Marks had tossed on a chair by the door—the envelope that had written on it the name of Maggie Whelan.

4.

"Who's Maggie Whelan?" Tatyana Rogov was lying on the floor, her body hugged by a yellow leotard, her legs pointed arrow-straight at the ceiling. With one swift movement, she lifted her torso completely upright and peered at Palmer through the posts of her thighs.

"How do you *do* that?" he said, amazed.

"Who's Maggie Whelan?" the answer came back. Tatyana's eyes, in her sculptured face, reminded Palmer of the eyes of a doe who looks up, startled, from a leafy glen to discover some jerk in a deer hunter's cap. Her eyes were alert, amused, afraid. The Russian temperament, Palmer thought, could accommodate a lot of strange contradictions.

"A reporter," he said. "She works on the show." He examined the barbells on the floor of the gym. They had to weigh at least eight hundred pounds. At the moment, their personal elevator service, the giant biceps of Gregori Yeshenko, were busily engaged in trying to remove a stubborn pop-top from a can of Coke. "I'll be back," Palmer said. He crossed the gym to where Arnold Kleber and the "On The Spot" crew were filming a Russian Olympic track star, who was frowning as he rapidly jogged in place.

Kleber said, "What?" and lowered the lens. Through mustache, beard, and aviator glasses, he grinned. "Whatcha got?"

"That," Palmer said, and pointed at Gregori who seemed to be cursing in Russian at the Coca-Cola can.

Laughing, Kleber pointed his minicam, moving in quickly on the giant at work. Palmer was already planning the line he'd record at the studio to cover the footage. "Ever been defeated by a pop-top can? Even the Olympic weight-lifting champ . . ."

"Hey, listen, Gregori," he said out loud. "You need any help?"

The big, bald Russian nodded and grinned.

"Keep it rolling, Arnie." Palmer winked at the cameraman. Once in a while a reporter got lucky like this and stumbled on a nifty button for his story. Palmer moved forward, flexing his muscles. Palmer, at thirty-six, was in good shape. A one-time quarterback with the Jets, he'd hung up his cleats when the doctor had told him, "You injure that disc of yours one more time and I can't even promise that you'll be able to walk, let alone play football." So Palmer had jumped when the job offer came: sports reporter for "On The Spot News." He'd been at the job since '76, gaining confidence, presence, style, and most important, a reporter's eye.

Palmer took the Coke from Gregori and grinned. He positioned it precisely for a medium close-up and tweaked at the tab.

It didn't budge.

Frowning slightly, he tweaked it again, this time harder.

Nothing.

Kleber, behind the camera, laughed. "Attaboy, Bobby. Show 'em the way."

The camera whirred.

Palmer pulled the tab as hard as he could. Nothing. And now he was starting to laugh.

"Keep laughing, you jerk." Kleber kept filming.

Palmer, suspicious now, examined the can, and read aloud, *"Made by the Boffo Novelty Corp. Things go better with a real can of Coke."*

Palmer broke up. "You sonofabitch," he said to Kleber. "The two of you rigged this."

Gregori laughed.

Palmer picked up a waiting mike. "So far, rumors have not been confirmed that Buffo is planning a branch in Peking."

"Not bad," Kleber nodded. "And as long as you're up, let's do some reverses."

Palmer nodded. Watching Tatyana move toward him, he smiled broadly and switched on the mike. "This is Robert Palmer. I'm standing in the Georgetown University gymnasium where members of the Russian Olympic team—now ending their week-long Washington tour—have been keeping in shape—" he glanced at Tatyana —"before they return to Moscow tomorrow. With me here now is Yuri Bulkanin." Tatyana was frowning; Bulkanin wasn't there. "Yuri, how do you feel about flying back to Moscow on the Concorde tomorrow?" Palmer moved the mike out of camera range, tilting his head as if he were listening. Tatyana stared at him as though she thought he was nuts. "Cut," Palmer said. Laughing, he turned to her. "We're shooting what we call a reverse," he explained. "I asked these questions when Yuri was here, but the camera was focused on him, not me."

37

"Oh. You mean you had your back to the camera and now you reverse your body to the front?"

"Something like that."

"Will you answer me one other question?" she said.

"Sure."

"The question I asked you before. Who is this woman who calls you this morning at a seven o'clock?"

Kleber looked up. "Give me a quarter and I'll go to the movies."

"Yeah." Palmer nodded. "Get lost for a while." Kleber moved off; he started shooting Gregori again.

Palmer put his hands on Tatyana's shoulders. "Darling," he said, "she's just a lady who works on the show. She's beautiful, bright, and probably seven other wonderful things, but it happens she's in love with somebody else, and it happens—" he sighed—"that I love you."

"But this Maggie, she calls three times in the morning."

"Hey—She's flying with us to Moscow tomorrow. The trip's all about the Olympiad, right? And Maggie doesn't know a damn thing about sports."

"So why is she coming?"

"The station wants a woman's perspective on Moscow, and I love it that you're jealous."

She was shaking her head. "That isn't nice."

"Why not?" He suddenly found that he was angry. "It just makes us even. I'm jealous too."

"Of what?" She was frowning.

"Of Moscow," he said. "You want to go back instead of staying with me."

"It's complicated, Robert."

"No. It's simple. When we met three years ago in Montreal, I kicked myself purple for letting you go. And then when the Olympics were set for Moscow, I thought, that's it. She'll never get out of Russia again. Not unless she wins the medal again. And then we sit and wait *another* four years. Listen, Tanya, it's easy. All we have to do is walk into the embassy—"

"No. And please not to ask this again." She was moving away, her dark hair bouncing.

"Then you don't have any goddam right to be jealous."

She turned, her doe eyes level and sad. "I don't have the right to leave my country. I'm not free to come and go as I choose. I'm not free to love you. But then . . ." She paused for a moment. "I'm not free to *not* love you, either." She shrugged sadly. "We'll be together in Moscow for a week. And again next year when you come to the Olympics. Don't be impatiently American, Robert."

He exploded. "Impatient! I've waited three years! Tanya?" But she'd turned, heading for the dressing room. Palmer just stood there, watching her go. He ran a hand through his sandy brown hair and down his face, and let out a sigh.

Kleber said, "Okay?"

Palmer shrugged, and sighed again. "Why couldn't I have fallen for an N.F.L. cheerleader?"

"Language barrier," Kleber offered, and Palmer laughed. Kleber checked his watch, and whistled. "I'll be late. I've got to get over to Maggie at Dulles."

"Yeah? What's at Dulles?"

"Our Concorde."

Palmer nodded. "You always get to airports a whole day early?"

"Funny. The plane is being delivered. Hoopla."

"Oh."

"Yeah, that's what *I* say." Kleber was yawning. "It's gonna be the icebox story of the night. The one where everybody gets up and goes to the icebox."

The sound man was packed and ready to go. Kleber waved.

"Hey," Palmer said. "Tell Maggie the answer to her question is 'three.' "

"What was her question?"

"How many rings in a three-ring circus?"

"I guess you're telling me it's none of my business?"

"I guess." Palmer grinned. "Give Maggie my love."

"Yeah? Well, I just drugged your wine. In twenty seconds—" he looked at his watch— "you'll be stricken with a wild, intemperate desire to run away with me to Spain." He studied her again. "How are you, Maggie? As blooming as you look?"

She felt herself flush. "I'm feeling just fine."

"What else are you doing? Aside from snitching on the Washington scene. I heard you got married to—"

"No," she said sharply. "You know how I feel about marriage."

He shrugged. "I know how you felt about marrying *me*. I didn't know it was a general credo."

"It was—is."

"Oh." He nodded slowly. "Well . . . if I promise not to marry you, how about having dinner tonight?"

"I can't," she said softly. "I'm busy tonight."

"And tomorrow?"

"I'll be in Paris tomorrow, on the way to Moscow. A pre-Olympics tour. It's also the maiden flight of F.W.A.'s Concorde, if it ever gets here, and I'm really—" She heard herself jabbering, and stopped.

He finished her sentence. "In love with someone else?"

She looked at him quickly. His eyes weren't on her. She followed his glance. He was looking at a man in a camel's hair coat.

"Yes," she said, thinking of David, and smiled. "What made you ask that?"

"I'm a detective." He turned to her. "Well. Have a good trip. I, uh—I guess I'll see you on the field."

She watched him as he walked away, then, shaking her head, she went to the bar.

"Champagne?" offered the barman.

"Yes," she said.

She looked at her watch: 3:25.

* * *

43

Pop! The bartender opened the bottle.

The champagne was Moët or Dom Perignon— something expensive. *"Pour la nouvelle année,"* the hostess had said. The hostess was a princess, or maybe a countess—something expensive. It was New Year's Day on the Île St. Louis, overlooking the Seine, in Paris. It was 1973.

Maggie, smiling, accepted the glass and gulped the champagne a little too quickly; it went the wrong way and she started to choke.

"C'est une jolie mort," said a man behind her, *"Mais, attendez."* He moved in quickly and slapped her on the back, hard. She stopped choking and looked at him.

"Ça va?" he asked. He looked American—the husky build and the coppery hair—but his French was flawless.

"Ça va," she said.

He grinned. "You're American."

"Ugh!" She flushed. "One word out of me and everybody knows."

"Why is it—" he began. The accent was Boston. She interrupted, "You're American too!"

He nodded. "Why is it," he repeated, "that Americans always want to sound like they're French?" He was frowning. "English is a much better language, much more clever and a lot more direct. What's your name, who are you, who did you come with, and are you in love with him?"

"That—" she started to laugh— "is direct."

In less than an hour he knew all about her: that she'd come from a dairy farm in Wisconsin; that she'd been here in Paris for almost a year; that she worked as a reporter for *Women's Wear Daily*; that her job consisted of covering fashion, "Of making headlines of hemlines and hats, and then, once in a while, reviewing a film and reporting What People Are Talking About."

"You mean, how they talk at the bar at the Ritz and the line for the *pâté de foie* at Fauchon." He said it with definite wry disdain.

She challenged him hotly. "Okay, McKeever. So what do *you* do?"

He looked at her. "What do I look like I do?"

She considered his clothes (not expensive), his eyes (inexpressive), and his manner (direct). "If I'd met you in Boston, I'd say you were a cop."

He laughed. "Not bad. I'm a private detective."

It was the first of the forty thousand lies he told.

They'd drifted from the party and gone to Select—a brasserie and a one-time Hemingway hangout. They went there often in the next few months. There were times when she didn't know why she saw him or what she saw *in* him. He was often evasive. He never said anything at all about his work, and when they talked about hers—it was work that she loved—he'd get that infuriating expression in his eyes, that slightly mocking "you'll grow out of it" look.

Once she'd exploded, "Damn you, McKeever. Can't you even try to *pretend* that you approve?"

"Uh-uh." He sat there shaking his head. "I spend most of my life pretending, Maggie. I need to have someone to be honest with."

"Oh. And you honestly couldn't approve of my life."

He smiled dryly. "The Skinny Life. Rags and bones and hanks of hair feeding on gossip. Get out of it, Maggie. You're better than that."

"It's a wonderful life. It's exciting. It's fun!"

He shrugged. "If you say so."

She accused him of being intolerant, humorless, jealous, ridiculous, harsh, and filled with the worst of all possible traits, the self-importance of being earnest.

And McKeever had tilted his chair back and laughed.

It was totally impossible to make him angry.

No. Not impossible. She'd once walked into his studio apartment and caught him on the phone, exploding in rapid French invective. When he hung up the phone, he wouldn't discuss it. By then, she knew what his job really was: counter-terror for the Paris station of the CIA. Before that, he said, he'd been stationed in Prague. He was there when it fell before Russian armor in the turning-point summer of '68. The men he'd worked with had been captured and slaughtered. The woman he'd lived with had been tortured and shot. He'd told her the story on a rainy Sunday at four in the morning, told her it was true, and that all the other things he'd told her were lies, and that most of what he'd tell her in the future would be lies. "Except that I love you. That'll always be true." In the darkness, he'd rolled over on the bed and looked at her. "That scares the hell out of you, doesn't it?"

"Love?"

"Not love. It's the 'always' that scares you."

She said, "I don't know what you're talking about."

And most of the time she didn't. She was a young twenty-four; he was an old thirty-one. She'd seen too little of the world; he'd seen too much of it.

She'd carried his baby for seven weeks when she had the abortion.

She told him nothing. If he'd known she was pregnant, he'd have tried to stop her. He'd have wanted the baby. He'd already proposed. And the last thing she wanted to do was get married. *Some* day, of course, she told herself, she would. And the picture faded and became hazy. A sunset, seen from a villa in Cannes, with indistinct children playing in the garden; a man who looked like Rossano Brazzi, silvery gray at the temples; a maid. The clearest person in the picture was herself. Poised, accomplished, forty at least. And certainly not any Mrs. McKeever.

Sometimes the image of Mrs. McKeever was painfully vivid: a woman in the park with a baby carriage, wondering if pork chops were getting too expensive, and whether her husband—right this minute—was dead or alive or something in between. Mrs. McKeever was a symbol of defeat, or worse, an enemy who had to be conquered. A dull, dowdy, worried woman who was planning the murder of Maggie Whelan.

And sometimes Maggie almost gave in, or saw how easy it would be to give in, how lying in McKeever's arms in the dark was almost like drowning, how drowners, seduced by the strength of the sea, stopped kicking and fighting and, after a while, got lightheaded, dreamy, relaxed . . . and were gone.

She'd gone to a clinic in Switzerland, "for a two week vacation." Upon returning, she didn't answer his calls. He'd persisted at first, and then let it go. And then he was gone—transferred, she'd heard from a friend, to Berlin.

A hand on her shoulder seemed to push her back to the present.

"Maggie, Maggie, forgive me, forgive me."

She turned; it was Kleber, scratching his beard. A minicam was perched on his shoulder. He sighed. "The traffic was brought to us straight from the zoo. It was out of its cage." He looked at his watch. "Well, I'm late, but the Concorde's later."

She looked at her watch: 3:26.

6.

"We are now exactly and officially late," O'Neill said cheerfully. "Right on the nose."

The altimeter needle was smoothly unwinding at the rate of five thousand feet per minute.

"ETA now three-forty-one."

At ten thousand feet, the Concorde banked gently to the left, slowed its descent on an altered heading, and dropped below a final layer of clouds.

"Le nouveau monde," Henri LeBec said. He motioned at the first faint glimpse of the coastline. "I wonder how long it took Columbus to get here."

"I don't know. But more than four hours, I bet." Metrand's dark eyes were scanning the instruments. "The first time I flew, it took seventeen hours to cross the Atlantic."

"Christ, when was that?" O'Neill hooted. "In 1920?"

"In 'fifty-one. The DC-6."

"The pterodactyl," O'Neill said, laughing.

"What's a pterodactyl?"

"A dinosaur with wings."

"Nineteen fifty-one's prehistoric to you?" Metrand turned around. "When were you born?"

O'Neill was grinning. "In 'fifty-three."

"That's obscene," Metrand said, scanning the console. "I was twenty-one then. And married."

"You were?" LeBec frowned. "You never mentioned—"

"She's dead," Metrand said, and wondered why the hell he'd mentioned her now. He'd buried her carefully.

Layers of clouds were below them again. The altimeter reading was eight thousand feet.

"So you were born," Metrand said quickly, "in the year supersonic travel was born."

"From a long and very dangerous labor," LeBec said pompously.

He was right, Metrand conceded. A long and dangerous labor it was. Ten years of test pilots breaking their heads on the obstinate, ultimate stone wall: the sound barrier. The phrase had been coined in the 1930s, and for twenty more years it had seemed to be true.

Metrand had studied the theory in school: airplanes flying at subsonic speeds send sound waves ahead of them, like messengers, yelling to the air up ahead, "Hey, air—move over! Plane's coming through!" And the air moves over and the plane moves through. But a plane that could travel as quickly as sound—so the theory went—would arrive at the same time as its telegram. There'd be no advance warning, nothing to scatter the air, to weaken its unyielding resistance. The air would fight back, become like a wall. Planes would disintegrate, crack up against it.

And that's what they did.

In 1946, after three years of trying to break the

barrier, of losing too many pilots and planes, research was canceled, at least in Britain—The risk was too great, the hope too slim—leaving the Americans, the born gamblers, to take on the project, and soon, to take the lead.

"In 'fifty-three," Metrand said aloud, "the first supersonic fighter came out. The F-100 Super Sabre. It hit mach one." He whistled. "That was something. The speed of sound. And then, five years later, the F-104 said double or nothing and won at Mach Two."

"McTwo was an Irishman," O'Neill said quickly.

Metrand just grunted. "Visor down."

"Visor down," O'Neill echoed. The visor came down, the pointed nose descending in preparation for the landing approach.

"Nose down—twelve and a half degrees."

The nose lowered.

The sky was dark.

The overhead radio crackled again.

They were cleared for landing.

Metrand looked down. The clouds around them were thick and gray; they were flying through a barrel of dirty feathers. He looked at the radar screen at his feet. It was clear sailing.

O'Neill was completing the final checklist: "Altimeter."

"Altimeter," LeBec repeated. "Six thousand feet."

"Airspeed."

"Airspeed two-one-two."

"Brake pressure."

"Brake pressure three thousand pounds."

The landing gear rumbled down into place: sixteen wheels with their double pairing of massive supports, and finally the dual-wheel nose gear. "Down."

"Autopilot."

"Off."

Metrand now had manual control of the plane, setting its nose on the characteristic steep-angled dive. The Concorde had neither spoilers nor flaps; its delta wing design, simple and clean, could master the air without any assistance.

Like a bullet shooting through a mountain of cotton candy, it cut through the clouds.

"Jesus!" The bubble of a hot-air balloon seemed to crash through the ceiling of the clouds up ahead, directly on the downward path of the plane. *"Nigaud!"* Metrand cursed, his hand on the throttles. "Gear up! Full power!"

They were seconds away from the goddam balloon, close enough to see there were three people in it. The balloon, too small to show up on the radar, was now too big, too big and too close; LeBec felt his fingernails dig at his palms; a cold-footed spider raced up his spine. But Metrand forced his will on the fast-diving plane, leveled it, and turned it sharply to the left.

"Mother of God." O'Neill made a sharp, windy whistle.

"Hell of a plane," Metrand said softly. "Nimble as a fighter."

"Concorde two-eight from Dulles Tower," the radio crackled. "Turn right on a heading of two-one-seven. Man, oh man," said the voice from the tower, "that's the flashiest fly-up I've seen in a year. We'll have to let you circle up there for a while, till we clear up the trouble."

"Roger, Dulles." Metrand rubbed his jaw. "What *is* the trouble?"

"Damned if I know. Seems the balloon doesn't want to come down. Looks like they're holding at five thousand feet. We can see 'em from the tower. They're over your runway. Climb to ten thousand, and hold your heading."

"Roger, Dulles." Turning, Metrand looked up at

51

LeBec, and frowned. "Hey, *copain,* you feeling okay?"

"Sure," LeBec said. What else could he say? Only one other time in his flying career had he felt as shaken as he did right now. And that time the plane he'd been flying had crashed—in exactly the way he'd pictured it crashing in a split-second vision an hour before. This time a vision had come to him too, just as Metrand made the swerving ascent to avoid the balloon. An image of war, missiles, flames. A deadly dogfight over an ocean. Impossible, he thought. Ridiculous. A left-over nightmare from some other night. But he thought about the terror attack in Iran. Air wars, it seemed, were still being fought. "Ridiculous," he said aloud.

"What's ridiculous?" Metrand looked up.

"Me," LeBec said. But the nightmare continued to ride through his mind.

He was glad he wasn't flying this plane back tomorrow.

They continued to circle, and started to climb.

He began to wonder if they'd come down.

7.

David Harrison stared at the portable television set that rested on the seat of his black limousine.

On the sun-baked tarmac at Mehrabad Airport, a 707 had burst into flames. A newscaster's voice said, "The plane was blasted with a ground-to-air missile as it banked for its final landing approach. Its altimeter reading was three thousand feet, when the oncoming missile—a Soviet SAM—shattered its cockpit. The plane exploded as it crashed to the ground."

Harrison shuddered and looked out the window.

It was the peak of the Washington rush hour. Traffic jams meshed at the corners; nobody moved in any direction.

Harrison stared at his chauffeur's neck. It wasn't a particularly interesting neck, but watching it was a form of meditation. He could concentrate fully on the thistle of hair, the single, circular chicken pox mark, and the twelve-degree angle described by the cap. He could lose his mind in such meaningless things and thereby prevent himself from losing his mind. Or so it was said.

It didn't work. His eyes went back to the television set.

"At Harrison Aircraft," the newscaster said, and again, David Harrison looked at his drone, pursuing the target.

"Man of the Year," the newscaster said. "That was the title conferred today by the board of the prestigious AAF—the American Aeronautics Foundation—on the man who invented this spectacular plane: Dr. David Harrison. Harrison plans to accept the award at a formal dinner tomorrow evening. However, there are those—"

He turned off his mind.

The traffic had started to move, and then, once again, had abruptly stopped. Up ahead, at the corner of 20th and K, the boxy, glittery Metal Building gave birth to another line of cars from its two-story subterranean womb.

Harrison laughed. Some days everything was one step foward and three steps back.

On the portable Sony, the newscaster said, "There was news in the air today and air in the news."

A Concorde landed on the field at Dulles.

"But it wasn't easy," a woman's voice said. "Delayed at first by the Harrison air test, and then by, of all things, a hot-air balloon . . ."

An orange balloon floated down to the field, and a couple of teenagers spilled to the grass. The balloon had AIRPEACE spelled out on its bag.

"Tossed by the storm and then lost in the clouds, the balloon had been heading for the Harrison Airfield. Its mission? To protest the Harrison drone."

"Dragonfly," Harrison said aloud. The least she could do was get the damn name right.

"I spoke to one of the men in the balloon: Don Cornelius, an engineering student at MIT." On the film, she stood with a curly-haired boy. "All right," she was saying, "now what's this about?"

"About two hundred million dollars, for openers." The kid looked grim. "That's what the Dragonfly's costing the public."

"The Pentagon seems to think it's money well spent."

"It's not their money," the boy said quickly.

"Are you complaining about the money or the drone?"

"Both. But I'll tell you what's wrong with that drone. It's a Frankenstein, that's what's wrong with it. It's a killer machine that can act by itself—it can't be controlled by the guys on the ground. You build yourself a thing like that and you've built yourself trouble."

The scene cut to the studio again, where a shaggy-looking boy announcer announced, "In reply, a spokesman from Harrison Aircraft—Dr. William Halpern, the chief designer of the Harrison drone—said, 'All the risks are minimal, and the plane's advantages far outweigh them."

Harrison poured a Scotch from a flask. *There are risks in everything, damn it,* he thought. *There are risks in automobiles and stoves and chimneys and bathtubs. So what does that mean? We should all stay at home eating uncooked hash, never taking a bath?* He looked at the set, resting his eyes, if not exactly his mind, on the fearful symmetry of Maggie Whelan.

The Sony did not do justice to her eyes, which seemed, on the set, to be an ordinary blue.

"Tomorrow night, I'll be reporting from Paris," she was saying crisply. "I'll tell you about my flight on the Concorde—the plane you just saw. It's turning out to look like an all-star flight: on the plane will be Olympics stars from America and Russia, and, of course, our own star sportscaster, Robert Palmer, who has been a pilot himself since the age of—" She laughed. "What was it you told me, Bobby? Three?"

Palmer, on camera, nodded. "That's right. The year I saw Dumbo and flew from a tree. I think we should mention that we'll be staying in Paris for only one day and then flying on to Moscow where we'll stay for a week. Then I flap my ears and fly Maggie home."

"In a final note," Maggie announced, "we've just learned that the government refuses to subsidize the B-1 Palmer."

"Ouch," Palmer said.

"And goodnight," Maggie added, "from 'On The Spot News.' "

Harrison turned the set off and smiled.

Maggie, he thought. *Maggie and her job. She jokes on the air, but she's deadly serious about her career.* Maybe that's why they got along so well. Maggie could understand Harrison's drive. If he said, "I'm working tonight, I can't see you," the words didn't trigger tantrums and tears. Unlike Ramona—the girl-before-Maggie—and unlike Mariah, who still, after seventeen years of marriage, could work up a sulk or a bitchy little dig. Mariah. He laughed. Just like the wind, she'd blown into town in—God, when was it?—1962. The Camelot years. A Boston friend-of-a-friend of Jackie's, she'd provided a link to the White House then. They'd attended concerts and a few dinners, and then Kennedy had offered him a White House post as advisor in assessing new Air Force projects. Harrison Aircraft itself, at the time, was still being run by David Harrison, Sr., and wasn't in the military hardware line, so there'd been no conflict of interest back then. And Jesus, he'd really wanted that post.

And then, Dallas.

And Johnson.

And the death of David Harrison, Sr.

And the death of David Harrison, Jr., he thought sardonically. *R.I.P.*

Only he hadn't had very much peace.

There was life after death—they were right about that—and he hadn't been sent to any hell on earth. He'd been sent directly to the winner's circle. Prizes, money, fame, success. It was quite a life.

Except for the minor detail that he was dead.

He studied the back of his chauffeur's neck, watched as a small droplet of sweat worked its way out from the edge of the cap and slid down the man's burly neck.

The car made a turn now, heading for Georgetown, and Harrison looked through the window again. They were climbing a narrow, curving street with brick sidewalks, blossoming trees, and small, colorful row houses—red, yellow, cinnamon, green. Another turn to a narrower lane and the townhouses here were older, Georgian, eighteenth century. The chauffeur parked next to one of them now, a dark house with a dark green door. He turned his head around and asked, "Shall I pick you up here at Miss Whelan's?"

"No. I'll manage," Harrison said. Quitting the car, he walked up the worn, red brick path and the three lopsided stairs.

The door had a polished lion's-head knocker. "This is my pet lion," she'd said, the first time she'd brought him here. "I warn you, he'll growl if he doesn't like you. On the other hand, he smiles if he does."

Harrison had stared at the lion for a moment. "In the interest of reliable reporting," he'd said, "I have to inform you he hasn't smiled."

"He will," she'd said blithely. "When he knows you as well as I do, he will."

She'd known him for almost a year at the time. Now she'd known him for almost two.

"And to hell with you," he said to the scowling lion. Using his key, he opened the door and entered a narrow, carpeted hall. He dropped his raincoat on the wooden coat tree and started to consider which he wanted most, a drink or a shower. Both, he decided, and walked up the stairs.

A half-hour later, showered, relaxed, and wrapped in a towel, and holding a drink in his hand, he stood in the bedroom and stared through the glass wall at the greenhouse. Attached to the bedroom, it was filled with greenery all year round. Sharon Wallis, the owner of the house, had decided that "gardens are terribly grim. In winter, I mean, they're deadly depressing—all bare and brown," so she'd put in a greenhouse at great expense, and then instantly married and moved to someplace in Central America, the new post of her ambassador husband. She hadn't been willing to sell the house, preferring to rent it, she'd brightly confided, "to some up-and-coming senator, you know? Someone who might end up in the White House and then my bed can be hung with a plaque that says, 'What's-His-Name Slept Here.'" Sharon had laughed.

But Harrison had introduced her to Maggie, and Sharon had decided to "lend" her the house, in exchange for keeping the furniture polished and the greenhouse green.

Or so Maggie thought. That Harrison deposited ten thousand dollars every six months into Sharon's account in Zurich was a factor he'd carefully never mentioned.

That Maggie had never suspected or asked was a sign of her lingering farm-bred innocence, the singular trait that Harrison cherished, or possibly even required, the most. Almost as much as he required the comfort and perfect privacy of Sharon's house. And since Maggie would never agree to be "kept," what Harrison kept instead was the secret.

It hurt no one; Maggie was happy, Sharon was happy, and Harrison himself was . . . content.

Now, through the window, he watched as Maggie got out of a taxi. Taking his drink, he moved to the bed—an antique rosewood four-poster with a ball-fringed canopy. "The surrey with the fringe on top," Maggie called it. It had taken them to warm, exotic places.

He finished his drink and waited for the sound of her key in the door.

8.

Lying in his arms on the canopied bed, watching him smoke a cigarette, she ran her finger down the bridge of his nose. "I love you," she said.

Smiling, he turned. "You're breaking the Eleventh Commandment," he said. "Thou shalt not commit love in adultery."

She laughed. It was ironic. One of the things she loved about David was that he didn't want her to love him, or at least that he didn't demand it. And this left her free. Free to love him. To love him freely, for his charm, his mind, his level honesty, and the perfect gift of the freedom itself.

The thing about adultery had never bothered her. She wasn't jealous of David's wife, or pricked with any needles of conscience about her. David's wife was a "Washington hostess." A party giver (for both parties), she collected the wielders of Washington power in her beautiful Billy Baldwin salon, where, the following morning, the rest of the world could admire their carefully tailored smiles in the society pages of the *Washington Post*. Her self-chosen job was public relations; private relations between them were zero.

"And you," she said, "are breaking the famous Twelfth Commandment."

"Which is?"

"Thou shalt honor thy mother-to-be."

"Huh?" He stretched, yawning out smoke. "Are you planning to be my mother?" he asked. "Now that would be incest and—" He stopped. He leaned on his elbow, watching her. "Maggie? What do you mean?"

"I'm pregnant," she told him, and grinned. "And I'm thrilled. Imagine what a wonderful baby we'll have. With his father's brains and his mother's . . . hmm . . ." She giggled. "Carelessness."

He frowned. "What happened?"

She shrugged. "The diaphragm slipped or something.The doctor said it might have been a Freudian slip. You know, like I forgot to put it in right because I wanted a baby."

"Do you?" he said. Squinting through smoke, he studied her, puzzled.

Or maybe he was worried.

She reached for his hand. "Don't worry, darling. I am, as they say, a big girl now—" she paused— "who's about to get bigger, I guess. I know what I'm doing. I want this child. And I don't expect . . . well, I don't expect anything from you. Really."

He was shaking his head slowly. "But what about your work? Your reputation?"

She watched him, amused. "You're referring, I suppose, to the Thirteenth Commandment: an anchorperson shalt not have a child."

"It reads, 'An unmarried woman shall not.' And I'm not sure how ready the world is, Maggie—"

"But I'm sure how ready *I* am, David. I—I

once—well, once I had an abortion, and I know—" she shook her head— "I couldn't do that again."

He frowned. "I thought you believed in abortion."

"I do. For anyone who wants to have one. But for me . . ." she remembered the months of depression, the unexpected longing she'd felt for the child, the guilty sadness that had never really left her. "Well, I just couldn't do it again. Besides, I want to have the baby, David. I want to have *our* baby."

"But what about your job? Won't they—"

"What? Fire me?" She laughed. "Of course not. I'll take a 'vacation' toward the end, but if anything, I think it would be good publicity." She smiled. "This is 1979."

He sighed. "I don't know what to say."

"Then shut up and kiss me."

"That's easy," he said, and kissed her, with a warmth that now, as always, quickened into passion.

And his telephone beeper on the night table buzzed. "Damn it," he said, and shut the thing off, then dialed his office on the bedside phone. "What's up?" he said, then waited, frowning. "If you're trying to be cryptic, Bill, you're succeeding. All right. I'll be there." He hung up the phone. "I'm afraid—"

She finished his sentence. "You have to go. You know, sometimes I feel like I'm sleeping with an egg, and just when it reaches the boiling point— ding, ding, ding, the timer goes off."

He laughed, moving quickly to the chair that held his clothes. "So—so you think I'm a hard-boiled lover?"

"A little." She watched him button his shirt. "Or at any rate, you're not romantic and mushy."

Slipping his shoes on, he sat on the bed, stroking her hair. "I wouldn't mind *you* getting mushy for a while. Why don't you do something sweetly senti-mental like cancel your flight and stay with me to-morrow? And come to the dinner where I get that award."

"Man of the Year." She was shaking her head. "At his side are his beautiful children, his wife . . . and his pregnant mistress. Now *that* is a picture for the cover of *Time*."

Grinning, he kissed her. "The American Dream. World on a string. The best of everything."

"Mmm. But then *I* want the best of everything too. My career, my trip on the Concorde tomorrow . . ." She kissed his neck. "My baby, and you."

"I see I come out on the bottom of the list."

"You're the top, my darling." She kissed him again. "But we both have our children to think about now."

He laughed. "You're a strange lady, you know. Maggie?" He picked up his watch from the table. "If there's anything—anything at all I can do—"

"There isn't. But of course if there is, I'll tell you," she said quickly.

As he moved from the bed, "There is."

He turned.

"If it's a boy, you can teach him to fly and play football and—"

"Hey! It's a little bit early for that."

"Well . . . 'this little piggie' will do for a while." She pulled up the covers, rubbing her eyes. There was packing to do, but it could wait for a while. She wanted a nap. "You going back to the office?"

"Mmm-hmm." Leaning over, he kissed her again, tenderly this time, on the tip of her nose. She won-dered if she'd ever get used to his looks—his strik-ing, incredibly handsome looks; she wondered if the baby would inherit those looks. And that mind. "Oh, David, I love you," she said.

He smiled. "Sweet Maggie. Have a wonderful trip."

"Mmm. Have a wonderful award," she said, "Man of the Year."

After he left, she drifted to sleep, thinking, "I'm having the Baby of the Year."

9.

Metrand had rented a car. He hadn't planned to. But on the airport bus that had taken the crew to their overnight rooms at the Marriott Hotel, he'd overheard Celeste confiding to O'Neill, "You know, I've never been to Washington, Pat."

"Well, then, you ought to rent a car," O'Neill said. "Take a tour of the city."

"I might," Celeste said.

So Metrand, on an impulse, had rented a car and, after a hurried shower and shave, had knocked on the door of room 701, the keys to a shiny Ford in his hand, *A Guide To The Capital* under his arm.

She'd opened the door, fresh from a shower, a terrycloth towel on her newly washed hair, and then stood there, staring, her head tilted, her brow slightly furrowed, her mouth in an O. And Metrand, who was rarely at a loss for words, who'd planned to say something offhanded and bright, found himself somehow unable to speak.

Maybe it was the lemon scent of shampoo, maybe the familiar polkadot robe, maybe just the soft, vulnerable mouth in its pleasing expression of perfect surprise, but whatever it was, it had taken him back two years, to the sunny apartment on the Rue Georges-Pitard.

She continued staring for another moment, then flashed him a quick, mischievous grin, and said rather tartly, "What took you so long?"

They did not see the White House, the Capitol, the Zoo, the Smithsonian Institution, the Lincoln Memorial, the Washington Monument, the Kennedy Center, or even the bellboy who delivered the food.

"McDonald's," she said. "My favorite food in the whole wide world." And they picnicked on the floor with the burgers and fries and chocolate shakes.

"I've missed you," he said.

She stopped laughing. "Well," she said lightly, "I missed you too. For a while, at least. It was difficult at first. I'd find myself stopping at the cleaner to pick up your suit. I actually did that a couple of times." She was stirring the straw around in her cup; she scooped up some chocolate froth and licked it. She shrugged. "But I got over that too."

"I'm sorry it didn't end better," he said.

"Ah! But you aren't sorry it ended. And no endings are ever happy. So what's the difference?"

"I never wanted to hurt you, Celeste. I just—"

"Didn't want to make a commitment. I know. Could we change the subject now, please? I won't make the error of loving you again, so you won't have to worry that you'll hurt me again."

He nodded, watching her licking her spoon. She'd changed into jeans and a soft yellow sweater; her hair was shiny, her eyes very clear, very matter-of-fact.

"And if *I* loved *you* again," he heard himself saying, "would that be an error?"

"On your part, yes."

He shrugged. *"D'accord."* He lit a cigarette with the hand that had wanted to reach out and touch her. He smiled. "Then I give you a choice for tonight. We go back to bed, just for old times' sake, or, uh . . . well, I still have the keys to the city." He held up the keys to the rented car.

"The city," she said. "I want to be friends again, Paul. That's okay. I—I always *liked* you. Even— even when I loved you." She laughed, then stood. "It's raining again. You'd better get a coat." She turned to him impishly. "And give me a minute to powder my lipstick and put on my nose. I'll meet you in the lobby in, say, ten minutes?"

All right, he told himself as he walked to his room. *Agreed:* D'accord. We'll just be friends. It was better that way, she was right. He couldn't make another commitment. He couldn't take it on again; he shouldn't try. Celeste was the closest he'd come to trying in the years since Angelique died. It was thirteen years since he'd stood in a downpour on the Grande Corniche, the curving, cliff-lined Riviera road where the screams still echoed—the scream of rebelling tires skidding on wet pavement, the scream of his wife . . .

She'd been twenty-seven.

She was still twenty-seven. She'd stopped, like a clock that could never be fixed and could never run forward. He'd been twenty-seven and then thirty-six and then forty-one and then forty-five, but Angelique would always be twenty-seven, frozen forever in a screaming moment, eternally lean and freckled from the sun.

He'd frozen there too.

Ironically, if people thought he'd changed, they thought he was more hot-blooded, less serious, lighter, more devil-may-care. He'd gone through women as a man might go through towns on a high-

67

way, stopping only for an overnight rest, some road-side nourishment, and then moving on. Where he was going, he'd never been sure; he'd only been certain he could not stay.

He'd stayed with Celeste three years ago, for almost a year. He'd been flying Mirages in the Sinai then, as part of a UN peacekeeping team. When his tour was nearly over, he'd decided to quit. They'd met in Tel Aviv, in a crowded pastry shop on Dizengoff Street. He'd seen her sitting at a table alone, a bright-looking girl in an Air France uniform. Metrand had just signed for a job at Air France. That was the ice-breaker.

Six weeks later he'd arrived in Paris, in the middle of an icy October storm. He'd phoned her from the public phone at Le Drugstore.

"Where are you staying?" she asked him.

"I'm not. Unless I can sleep standing up in a booth. I've been calling hotels for an hour and a half. Everything's booked. What's going on?"

"Auto convention."

"Oh." Sighing, he shook his head. "Well, I tell you, I feel like the three bears. They're not only sleeping in my goddam bed, they're eating my porridge. I can't even get myself a meal in this town. It's a two-hour wait for a table, they tell you. Even at Le Drugstore."

She was silent for a moment, then she laughed. "Are you subtly asking me to cook you a meal?"

"I'm asking, if I brought some food to your house, would you lend me a knife and a fork and a chair. Have you eaten?"

"No."

"All right, how about it? And afterwards, I'll call some hotels from your house."

He'd brought the food, they'd picnicked on the floor, and by the time he got around to phoning hotels it was seven months later, the beginning of summer. They'd gone on a weekend trip to the south, to visit Celeste's sister in Cannes. And on the way back, she drove the car. And drove the Corniche. And everything snapped.

The bedside telephone started to ring, jarring him suddenly into the present. It was the hotel switchboard. What time did he want to be awakened tomorrow—five or six? The note he'd left at the desk wasn't clear.

"Six," he said. The flight was at nine; he'd have to check in by 7:15, to check out the traffic from here to Paris, the weather conditions, the load reports, and then make the final captain's decisions, and file the flight plan with traffic control. In the back of his mind, he'd pictured a pleasanter way to wake up than the strident jangle of a bedside phone: a hand on his shoulder, a voice in his ear, the minty taste of a toothpaste kiss.

Still, she was right. It was better like this. He looked at his watch. He'd wasted five minutes. He ran his fingers quickly through his hair and reached for his coat, turning at the sound of a knock on the door.

"Ah! Tu as changé d'avis," he shouted, expecting Celeste, and opened the door on a tall, burly, tough-looking man, who stood there awkwardly shifting his weight.

"Uh . . . you're Captain Metrand?" he said.

Metrand nodded.

"I'm, uh, Joe Patroni," said the man. "I'll be, uh, flying with you tomorrow as your first officer? Anyway, I just got in and I thought I'd say hello. Maybe have some dinner together if you, uh . . ." He shrugged.

"Oh," Metrand said. "I—it's a pleasure to meet you, Captain." He shook the man's hand. From everything he'd heard, this Joe Patroni was a hell of a pilot—the senior man at FWA. "But you see, the problem is, I—"

"Have other plans," Patroni said quickly, and grinned. "I don't blame you. As much as I wanted to meet you, Metrand, I'd *also* rather be with a beautiful girl. Come on." He made a quick two-handed shrug. "If you're going to the lobby, I'll, uh, copilot you down."

In the elevator, Metrand looked over his American copilot. Patroni had a big, truck driver's face. Brown-eyed, white-haired, he looked more like Metrand's idea of a football coach than a senior pilot. He was easily six foot three, but he didn't seem very easy about it, didn't know what to do with his hands or his eyes. He was shy. He cleared his throat. "I, uh, I'm looking forward to the flight tomorrow."

Metrand nodded. "You trained on the simulator?"

"In Toulouse."

"Not much of a town."

"Good bouillabaisse, though." Patroni slapped his gut with the flat of his hand. "And the bread! Bread's my weakness," he added, as the elevator opened.

Celeste stood in front of it, smiling at Metrand. "And is that *your* weakness?" Patroni laughed.

Metrand said flatly, "That's our flight attendant. Celeste Maigon—Captain Patroni. The Captain's—"

"Flying with us tomorrow. I know." Celeste shook Patroni's hand. "Captain." She smiled. "I've heard a lot about you."

"Oh." Patroni seemed to color at that. "Well." He cleared his throat. "Can I give you two a lift? I've got a car out front and I—"

"Thanks," Metrand said, "but I've got one too."

"He's showing me the sights," Celeste added quickly. "I've never been to Washington."

"Oh," Patroni said, and then said nothing, and Metrand said, "Well . . ." and took Celeste's arm, but Patroni said, "Too bad everything's closed. I mean, all the buildings close around five. But what you might do—I mean, after you take a quick look around—well, there's this cabaret up in Georgetown, and they do this kind of cute political revue—"

"Would you like to come with us?" Celeste interrupted.

"Oh, well, I wouldn't want to— No, three's a crowd."

"Nonsense," she said. "We insist. Don't we?" She smiled at Metrand and tossed him a pointed kick in the shin.

Metrand smiled nicely and said, "Well, of course. Please."

Celeste said, adding insult to injury, "Yes. Paul and I, we are simply good friends."

Patroni perked up and grinned at the news. "Well, then." He took Celeste's arm in his. "In that case, we'll go like the three musketeers." He looked at Metrand. "What were their names?"

"D'Artagnan, Delilah, and the third was De Trop."

Celeste gave Metrand a quick, angry look.

Metrand smiled.

"Let's go," Patroni said.

10.

Maggie woke suddenly and sat up in bed, feeling a momentary flicker of panic before she rolled over and looked at the clock. It was 9:03, and much too dark to be nine in the morning. She hadn't overslept, just napped. She stretched, moaning long and luxuriously, and then yawned at the canopy over her head. On the printed blue and white muslin toile, dozens of flocks of little blue sheep wandered away from a "little blue peep," as David had once called her—a careless shepherdess who sat on a rock, gathering bunches of little blue flowers.

In the year and half she'd been living in this house, she'd spent only two full nights here with David. Once in a while she'd allowed herself to dream about his getting a divorce. But even in a dream, she didn't really want the job of being his wife. And it would be a job. A full-time job. Giving all those parties and smiling at generals, and being tactful instead of incisive. She had the best of him this way—the best of him, and the best of herself. And still, she had to admit, there were nights when she lay awake, counting her little blue sheep and wondering what the hell was wrong with her life. And even when she lay awake counting her blessings, the count still didn't tally. Something was wrong.

But whatever it was, there wasn't really time to think about it now. *Up,* she told herself. *Things to do. Wash hair, pack clothes, what else? Something else . . .* She yawned. Broken pane of glass in the greenhouse. *Right. Leave a note for the gardener to fix it.*

Up.

She opened the window wide, and leaned on the sill. The pavement on the street below was wet, washed by the rain, glowing slightly in the light of the streetlamp. Empty, without any people or cars, it might have been a street scene from 1780; any minute a carriage would drive down the block, hooves clopping, wheels clattering.

A yellow Mazda drove around the corner, very sleek, very 1979, breaking the spell. She turned from the window and, yawning, opened the big glass door to the greenhouse and studied the broken pane. It was right on the sunroof, five panes over, in front of the latch. Well, Juan would see it. She should leave him a check. She wondered how much the glass would cost. Twenty dollars or a hundred and twenty; it was hard to guess what *anything* cost these days.

She turned at the unexpected sound of the doorbell. Who'd drop by without calling her first? The bell rang again. Annoyed, she reached for her robe on the chair.

The bell rang again, more insistently now.

"I *hear* you," she shouted. "Hold it. I'm coming."

At the door, she peered through the peephole and

73

frowned. A thin, balding, rabbity man stood on her doorstep. "Who is it?" she asked.

"Please," he said hoarsely. "Open the door."

He didn't exactly look like a thief; on the other hand, he looked just a little bit nuts. His eyes were darting around like flies; he kept looking over his shoulder at the street.

"Who is it?" she repeated. "And what do you want?"

"Please. Let me in. I'll—" He sighed, then went on in a burst, "My name's Carl Parker. I'm the sales director at Harrison Aircraft. I *must* talk to you. Quickly. Please."

From Harrison? "Oh. Just a second." She closed the peephole, opened the door.

The man checked the street, then entered furtively, closing the door behind him. He coughed. His suit was damp from the rain. He looked pale, exhausted. And nuts, she decided. He chewed on his lip, then rubbed at his jaw, and she began to regret that she'd let him come in. "I'm sorry," he said. "I would have called first, but your number's not listed." He was catching his breath.

She nodded. "What's your problem, Mr., uh—"

"Parker. Carl Parker." He looked up quickly; his dark eyes blinked. "Those papers—those papers you have—they're mine."

Uh-oh, she thought, *right off the wall.* "I—I don't know what you're talking about."

"The papers. The blueprints. Please! You have to—" He blinked again. "Didn't you open the envelope?"

"No. What envelope?"

"Didn't you get it?" He grabbed her by the arm. She was frightened now, really frightened. How *stupid* she'd been to open the door! "No," she said, trying to keep her voice calm. He was standing with his back to the outside door; it was slightly ajar but

74

his body blocked it. If she had to run, she'd have to run out the back. "And I still don't know what—"

"This afternoon. One of the reporters from 'On The Spot News' was at Harrison Aircraft."

"Yes. So?"

"He had an envelope with him."

"And?"

The man was clenching his fists; his knuckles were white. In fact, he seemed more frightened than she was. "Look, there were papers I put in that envelope. Papers I had to get out of there fast. I guess—I guess it was a dumb thing to do, but it seemed like a chance, like my *only* chance, and it worked. At least he got out of there with them. And you have them now. You *must* have them now." It was more like a plea.

"I? *I* don't—" And then she remembered. The envelope switch. She'd gone to the airport with Jeffrey's envelope and he'd gone to Harrison Aircraft with hers. Her name was on it. This man must have seen that. She shrugged. "Jeff never gave me the envelope back. I *don't* have your papers, whatever they are. If you gave them to Jeff, then he still has them." Frowning, she stared at him levelly now. A hundred suspicions clashed in her head.

Carl Parker ran his hands through his hair. "He didn't know he had them when he left the building. I put them in the envelope without his knowing. I tried to phone him, but first they told me he was still on the air, and then they told me he'd gone out of town. On assignment." He looked at her bleakly. "Is that true?"

"Yes. Now, I think you'd better start from the top. What kind of papers were they, and why did you—?"

"Listen! Please. There isn't much time. I know I'm being followed. The papers have—they have information I wanted to bring to the FBI. It's proof."

"Of what?"

"Of illegal arms sales. I wanted—"

"Hold it! Illegal arms sales? What are you—?"

"Weapons. Weapons, Miss Whelan. Rifles, grenades. Arsenals sold to terrorist groups."

"By Harrison Aircraft? You're wrong. They don't even *make* grenades."

"No. But Harrison Industries does. Small arms, rifles, launchers, grenades. They're made by Armuco in lower Manhattan, a subsidiary of—"

"Harrison?"

"Yes." Parker glanced through the window behind him. He rubbed at his chin with the back of his hand. "I might as well tell you the whole story now. I, uh, don't think I did too well as a spy." He laughed ruefully. "In movies it turns out better than this. I know—I know they know what I've done. They're after me. Look, when you get the envelope, take it to the FBI. There's proof. Not only of the illegal sales, but there's also—" He stopped. "Look, the authorities will know what it is, and it's *urgent*."

"You have to be wrong," Maggie said. "I don't believe this. I don't understand it and I don't believe it. If it's true, you ought to go to David Harrison. I'm sure he'd be the first to—"

"He *was* the first. The first to make millions by arming terrorists. And I have the proof."

She was shaking her head. "I'm sorry, Mr. Parker. It doesn't make sense. David Harrison selling arms to terrorists? Why? He couldn't possibly agree with their actions. He's dedicated to saving lives, and he certainly doesn't need the money. So why?"

"I don't know. I don't know why. I just know he did."

Watching the nervous little man in her hallway, she remembered a conversation with Roger Arden, the head of David's security corps. Arden, who'd worked for the FBI, had told her, "Spies aren't movie-star spies. They're not James Mason and Cary Grant. They're usually sad, jerky little guys, but they're carefully trained and terribly smart. And they're better actors than Mason and Grant."

So maybe this nervous act was just that—an act. This improbable story—and it *was* improbable— could just be a cover to convince her to help. If he'd smuggled secrets out of David's building, the man who was after him could well be Arden. The alternative was that he was telling the truth, and that would make David— Impossible. No. She knew David. But still, her job was to look for the truth.

"If these papers exist," she said to him slowly, "there's a chance they'll be at the office right now. Jeff might have tossed them on his desk. To begin with, I think we ought to go there and look."

He was shaking his head. "I don't—I don't think I should go there with you. I'm being followed."

"By whom?"

"I don't know."

"Did they follow you here?"

"They tried. But I shook them."

"All right," Maggie said. "Then we'll take my car. Just give me a minute to throw on some clothes."

Shrugging, he nodded. "All right. If you say so."

"I say so." She turned and walked up the stairs.

As she reached the landing, she heard the sound. It was simply a dull compression of air, followed by a strangled gasp. She turned as Parker, lurching, blood-spattered, fell to the floor, and, almost paralyzed with fear, she caught a glimpse of the man at the door with the gun. Screaming, she raced up the rest of the stairs, as shots gouged into the stairwell around her. She got to her bedroom, slammed the door and locked it, then listened for sounds on the stairs. Nothing. Maybe he hadn't followed her. She ran to the telephone and fumbled with the dial, before she realized the phone was dead. Now she could hear his feet on the stairs and the hollow whisper of the silenced shot as he blasted the lock.

Quickly she ran through the greenhouse door, and crouched under a shelf of plants. Through the big glass wall, she stared at his feet, watching as they moved toward the open window. Maybe he'd think— But he wouldn't, didn't. The feet, in their shiny black shoes, came back and planted themselves on the carpet. She moved quickly, quietly, keeping her body low. She reached for a shovel. He moved through the door. She saw him clearly now,—a clean-cut, well-dressed, good-looking man, with a silenced revolver gripped in his hand. His eyes moved quickly through the darkened room with its pungent scent of roses.

He turned.

She moved, swinging the shovel straight at his gun hand. She missed, as he blocked the move with his arm, but the gun was lowered, and she swung at his knees. He yelped, losing his balance, and barrelled into a table of plants. As it crashed to the floor, he went down, his gun jumping out of his hand like a frog.

She leapt for the ladder that led to the roof, and scrambled up as he climbed to his feet. He yanked at the hem of her robe, tearing it, as she pounded the broken pane, sending daggers of glass raining down on his head. It stopped him for a second—the second she needed to undo the latch. It was raining and the glass was slippery and wet, but she climbed through the open sunroof and screamed, "Help me. Somebody. Get the police."

A woman moved toward the yellow Mazda parked at the curb. She turned, looked up, seemed to freeze.

"Help!" Maggie screamed, and then lost her balance as the man on the ladder got a grip on her leg. She kicked at his face and felt herself slide straight down the slippery, slant-angled roof, catching herself at the final second. Gripping the metal rain gutter now, she hung suspended in the air. And she heard him moving carefully toward her.

11.

In this temple, as in the hearts of the people for whom he saved the union, the memory of Abraham Lincoln is enshrined forever. Celeste read the words on the wall. The towering statue of Abraham Lincoln, lit by floodlights, seemed to look down directly at her. The famous, homely American face seemed almost alive.

"And, you know, that statue," Patroni was saying, "was done by a man named Daniel French. The French were the city planners of this town. L'Enfant, Lafayette." Flushing, he shrugged and then looked at Metrand. "I've been reading too many guidebooks, I guess." He looked at the guidebook. "So where would you like to go after this? Capitol Hill? Or do you want to take a look at the FBI?"

"You certainly know your way around town," Metrand said dryly. He liked Patroni—but not tonight. He admired Lincoln—but not tonight. He did not want to look at the FBI.

"The FBI," Celeste was saying.

"It's between the White House and the Capitol. There." Patroni pointed at the Washington Monument. "That way. Up Pennsylvania."

"Swell."

They went up Pennsylvania Avenue, then stood in front of a massive, block-long concrete building.

"Derives from the work of Le Corbusier," Patroni was reading.

"Like hell it does," Metrand said sharply. "It's sterile, ugly. Le Corbusier made buildings in France that are monumental. This one is just monumentally bad."

Patroni looked at him. "You know about architecture?"

"No, but I know what I do not like." Metrand looked again at the huge, square, almost brutal building. The three-story columns that fronted the street seemed to dwarf the tall, redheaded man who, lighting a cigarette, walked through the door. Passing Metrand, he delivered a quick, disinterested look and then walked to a car waiting at the curb. He seemed to have trouble finding his keys, and fumbled in his pocket. The human element, Metrand thought dryly. Out of that big, monolithic bluff, a human being who can't find his keys.

It was starting to rain. "Come on," he said. "I'll circle you around the Capitol once, and then—" he yawned and looked at his watch— "I'll drop you off at that Georgetown club."

"Don't you want to come?" Celeste asked.

"No." He looked back at her. "I want to go to bed."

12.

"And then what happened?" the lieutenant asked.

Maggie was watching the medical examiner as he examined the bloody corpse in her hall. She shivered.

"Miss Whelan?" the lieutenant repeated.

"What?" she looked up at him. "What did you say?"

"And then what happened? After you called for help from the roof."

"I slid, and I was kind of left hanging, you know. The woman on the street rang a fire alarm and the killer got scared, I guess, and he ran."

"And you managed to lift yourself back to the roof. And then?"

"I got to my bedroom and screamed."

"Why?"

"It just seemed like a good idea."

The lieutenant looked at her.

Maggie sighed.

He nodded. "You're making a joke," he said.

"Not a very good one, I guess. I'm sorry."

"Was there someone in the room? Is that why you screamed?"

"Forget it." Maggie sighed. "There was no one in the room. Haven't you ever just felt like screaming?" She looked at the lieutenant. "Of course you haven't. Well, anyway, I screamed and then put on my coat, and then . . . about a dozen policemen arrived."

"Who've already asked you a thousand questions."

"Yes."

"And you're tired."

"Exactly."

"I see." Lieutenant Dobbs was a middle-aged man. His eyes were pouchy, the skin on his jaw was sagging. "And you tell me you want to leave town tomorrow."

"I must." She looked at him and shivered again. "Please. It's my job, and it's terribly important. And I've already told you everything I know."

She hadn't, of course; she wondered if he knew that. But how *could* he know? And how could she tell him what Parker had said? If it wasn't the truth—and it *couldn't* be the truth—she'd be ruining David, or putting him under tremendous suspicion, over nothing at all.

But what if it were true?

She looked at the corpse and shivered again.

". . . case of shock," the lieutenant was saying.

She looked at him.

"I said," he repeated, "I think you might have a slight case of shock. You're shivering. Do you have any brandy in the house?" he frowned. "Or maybe you should call a doctor."

"No. I'm all right." She was shaking her head,

but then she stopped and said, "Yes. I think— yes. You're right. I should call a doctor."

In the kitchen, alone, she picked up the phone and dialed. "Dr. David Harrison, please," she whispered. "It's urgent."

Harrison swiveled around in his desk chair. Halpern lit a pipe and leaned against the wall, running a hand through his curly gray hair. Arden, his holster bulging in his armpit, paced through the office, shaking his head.

"How could the bastard have done it?" Arden said. "I've got security gadgets up the kazoo. I've got seventeen guards—"

"He did it," Halpern said. "He ripped off secret blueprints from the files. And all that matters now is where the hell are they?"

"Yeah," Arden said. "Well, he didn't have them when he left the building, so he must have got them out through somebody else. Damn it!" He turned.

Harrison frowned. "You went over the photographs you take at the door?"

"I'm not totally stupid," Arden said hotly. When Arden got angry, it was something to see. His square-jawed face turned a fiery red. "I also put a couple of guys on his tail."

Halpern looked at Harrison, then back at Arden. "And?" he said.

"Nothing so far. Last I heard, he hadn't gone home and his wife's not there either." Arden checked his watch. "I'll be getting another report in an hour."

Halpern shrugged. "You're doing your best. That's all we can ask."

"I still think I ought to call some guys at the Bureau. They can give us—"

"Not yet," Halpern said quickly. "If we can handle this ourselves, we're in a better position.

With the Dragonfly contracts, the last thing we need is a scandal that shows a security leak." He narrowed his eyes. "I'd say that's the last thing *you* need, too. We'd have to let you go, and it doesn't make the hottest resumé item to——"

"Yeah, yeah, yeah," Arden said dully. He paced to the door. "So I'm looking for a file slugged 'Project Why.' And I'd like to know *why*, if it's so damn secret, you leave it in your office instead of——"

"I'd *thought* my office was safe," Harrison snapped. "With all your gizmos and seventeen guards——"

"All right," Arden said. "Message received." He opened the door. "I'll give you a report as soon as I get one."

Halpern just nodded. "Sweet dreams," he said flatly, and waited till the door had closed with a click. "So?" he said to Harrison.

"So all we do is wait."

"If Cooper——"

"And forget about 'ifs.' 'Ifs' can drive you crazy. Believe me, Bill. Just go home and relax."

"Relax? How the hell——?"

Harrison laughed. "Then go design a plane. Keep your mind off your worries." He lit a cigarette, nodding. "Speaking of planes you designed, the Dragonfly test tomorrow ought to show——"

The telephone rang.

"Cooper," Halpern said.

"Possibly." Harrison picked up the phone.

Maggie, in a whisper, said, "David?"

Harrison frowned, and shook his head at Halpern. "Maggie? Anything the matter?"

"I . . . don't know. I don't think so. I hope not. David—I've got to talk to you."

His frown deepened. "Why are you whispering?"

"There are seven policemen standing in my hall."

"There are *what*?"

"Nothing compared to what *was* in my hall. Are you acquainted with a man named Carl Parker?"

"Parker?"

Halpern wheeled, and then froze, staring at Harrison.

Harrison scowled, but said very levelly, "Yeah. Sure I am. He's my sales director. Why? What about him, Maggie?"

"He's dead."

"Dead?"

Halpern bit his lip.

Harrison swiveled around in his chair, facing the window. "What do you mean about Parker being dead?"

"I mean he was shot to death in my hall."

"In . . . *your hall?*"

Halpern buried his face in his hands.

"David, stop repeating everything I say. I haven't got time—"

"What happened?"

"I don't know. A man rushed in here and shot him in the chest. And then tried to shoot me."

"What was Parker doing—"

"Don't you want to ask me if he shot me, David?"

"Maggie. Darling. You don't sound shot. If you were wounded, you'd be in a hospital. Darling—" Harrison looked at Halpern again— "this is very—strategically important," he went on. "Please tell me what Carl Parker was—"

"He said he had papers. Documents, David. Documents proving a place called Armuco was selling munitions to terrorist groups."

"Armuco?" Harrison said. "What's that?"

"He said that you own it."

"News to me. What else did he say?"

"That was pretty much it. Except he seemed to think that I had the papers."

"And do you?"

A pause. "Of course not," she said. "If you don't own Armuco, the papers don't exist. Why did you ask me if I had them, David? *Do* they exist?"

Harrison weighed the question for a moment.

"Do they, David?"

"No." He paused. "But maybe I should let you in on the truth. Some other papers exist, Maggie. I think he may have stolen some blueprints from our files. Listen—did you tell the police this story?"

"No. Oh, David. Do you think I'd tell them without telling you first?"

"Good. Keep it quiet, honey. This is top security. It's not the province of the Metropolitan Police, and we don't want a leak. If we have to call anyone, we'll call the Bureau, but I'm still half hoping we can handle it ourselves." He looked up at Halpern, who nodded slowly. "But if any of their agents come nosing around, do us both a favor and stay uninvolved. You don't know the real story, and the one you *do* know could damage us both. And the real story, Maggie, could compromise the whole Dragonfly program."

"I wouldn't do anything to hurt you, David. Or to hurt your work. I know what that project means to you, darling." She was silent for a moment. "Who killed him, David?"

"What?"

"Who killed Parker?"

"How would I know?"

"It wasn't . . . Arden? Or one of his men? I mean, if you were trying to track down the blueprints . . ."

"We were. We are. And we'd certainly be clever enough not to shoot him before he could tell us what he did with them, Maggie. I mean, we wouldn't shoot him at all, but— Look, Parker must have had a deal with someone who wanted to buy those papers. God only knows who he might have been dealing with. Anyone from the KGB to the Mafia."

"David? I can hear them in the dining room now."

"Who?"

"The police." She was whispering again. "I think I'm under quarantine or curfew or something."

"What time does your plane leave? Or won't they let you go?"

"They will. It's at nine. Why?"

"Why? My God, honey, after what you've been through? I want to see you off, make sure that you're safe."

"Oh, darling." She sighed. "What a terrible mess this is. I wish I could be with you. Oh, boy. Would I like you to hold me right now. Oh, damn it. Good-bye, darling," she whispered. "Till tomorrow."

She hung up the phone and reached for the brandy the lieutenant had prescribed.

He was leaning in the doorway. "You think you could answer a few more questions? There's an officer here who—"

She tilted her head. The officer was—

"Luke?" she said. "What are *you*—?"

"CIA," he said to her quickly. "Calls Instantly Answered." He smiled at her and shrugged. "Somebody told me you'd called from the roof."

"I—"

"That's expensive brandy you're spilling. Sit down," he ordered.

She stared at him.

"Sit."

She sat at the table, and he sat across from her. Dobbs walked out to the living room again. McKeever kept watching her, frowning. "Drink up," he said, and lit a cigarette. Watching her drink, he rubbed at the back of his neck with his fist.

She drank, and felt the burning lift of the brandy.

"So," he said slowly. "Tell me about it."

She wondered what he knew. If he was here at all, he had to know something. But what? She took a breath and squared her shoulders. "He told me his name was Carl Parker. He told me he worked at Harrison Aircraft. Then he blathered about some—" She stopped abruptly.

"About some what?" He studied her now with cool gray eyes.

She'd never been able to lie to McKeever. The best she'd ever been able to do was avoid him when she wanted to avoid the truth, as she'd done in Paris.

She avoided his eyes. "About some kind of trouble. He seemed to be very excited about it. I couldn't make sense out of what he was saying."

"And what—exactly—verbatim—did he say?"

She swallowed more brandy. As a kid in Wisconsin, she'd once seen a movie where, whenever the hero did not like the scene, he rubbed on a locket and just disappeared. She did not have a locket, but she certainly did not like the scene—lying to Luke, lying to the government. But still, since she *knew* the story was a lie that could hurt David and help no one . . . "Luke, I—I really can't remember exactly. Just that there was some kind of trouble."

"At Harrison?"

"I suppose."

"Uh-huh. And why do you suppose he'd be telling that to you?"

"I don't know. Well . . . maybe because . . . well, after all, I *am* a reporter."

He nodded. "And David Harrison's mistress." He said it in a completely neutral voice.

"Parker didn't seem to be aware of that fact."

"Uh-huh."

"He honestly didn't, Luke."

McKeever nodded. "Go on," he said.

She looked in his eyes and wished she could tell him the rest of the story. "There isn't much more. He sort of alarmed me. He seemed to think he was being followed. He said something like, 'They're after me,' and he was so excited, I really couldn't tell if 'they' were little green men from Mars or—" She shrugged. "Well, anyway, I started to walk up the stairs, to call the police." McKeever shot his glance at the phone in the kitchen. She added quickly, "I wanted to be able to talk to them in private. I mean, I didn't know if he was crazy or not. And then somebody rammed through the door and shot him. And I ran. And the killer chased me and—"

"Yeah. I know the rest." He stubbed out his cigarette. "And that's all you know?"

She nodded, then continued, "Luke, will you tell *me* something now? What's this about? Why are you here?"

He laughed. "Come on, Maggie."

"Were you following Parker? Do you think—do you think he was some kind of spy?"

McKeever cocked his head. "Do *you* think so, Maggie?"

"I don't know. I thought, well, if *you're* here . . ." She let it trail off.

He didn't pick it up. But of course he wouldn't.

Then, suddenly, he said, "It's routine, Maggie. Parker worked for Harrison Aircraft. Harrison holds a lot of military blueprints. Parker, it seems, was assassinated. Kind of makes the government start to get curious."

"*Your* branch of government?"

"Sure. We're working with the Bureau on this. Just a routine investigation of Parker."

She nodded slowly. "Yes, but why *you?* I mean, aren't you still working counter-terror?"

He was shaking his head. "Honey, that was six years, two bullets, and five thousand miles ago. No. I'm just working at a Washington desk. Kind of a general assignment desk."

"Oh." But she wasn't sure she believed him. Not that he wasn't convincing. McKeever could convince you it was snowing in June. And that's why she wasn't sure she believed him.

"Tell me more about Parker's killer," he said. "I've got the description you gave the police. Tall, clean-cut, good-looking blond guy in a raincoat. What kind of raincoat, Maggie?"

"Tan. A trench coat."

"You know about clothes. An expensive trench coat?"

She thought, then nodded. "Yes, in fact. I'd say a Du Mars."

"What the hell's that?"

"Claude Du Mars. A designer."

"Oh. An expensive designer raincoat."

She nodded. "And his shoes. When I was hiding under the table, I got to see an awful lot of his shoes. They were French. Expensive. Souliers Parc."

"Uh-huh."

She thought. "I think he might have been a foreign agent."

He looked at her; he seemed to be biting a smile.

She flushed. "Well, he *looked* like a foreign agent. I mean, he didn't look like a Mafia goon. He wasn't the type."

"In twenty seconds you decided his type? Baby doll, the one thing you never did well was to size up character."

She glared at him.

"Rolf Von Steiner," he said. "Remember him? Jesus, you were so knocked out with his charm—"

"That was six years and five thousand barons ago."

"He was still the biggest swindler ever to hit France."

"Are we arguing ancient history now?"

"We aren't arguing." McKeever rose. "I think it's just as well you'll be going out of town. The lieutenant will be leaving some men here tonight, and they'll see that you get safely to the airport tomorrow."

"Why?" She looked at him. "It's over, isn't it?"

McKeever just stood there, shaking his head. "Sometimes you remind me of Nancy Drew."

"As I remember, she wasn't a bad detective."

"Right. For a fictional twelve-year-old. Maggie, you saw that assassin's face. That alone would be enough to put you in danger. But secondly, the guy was on Parker's trail. Now if *I* were the killer, I might suspect that Parker had told you something." He looked at her levelly. "I mean something more than he actually told you."

"Oh." She nodded, and lowered her eyes.

"I want to go up and take a look at your roof. The police will be sending an artist over here. See if you can help him do a drawing of the killer."

She nodded.

McKeever started to leave, then turned back. "One more question," he said to her briskly. "Strictly personal and unofficial."

"Yes?"

"Are you really in love with Harrison?"

"Yes."

He nodded. "Have a good trip."

13.

Metrand was staring at the ceiling in the dark. It was one of those nights when the ticking of his watch was keeping him awake. And the thought of Celeste. She was playing a game with him, of course, getting in a little sweet revenge.

He undoubtedly deserved it, but that didn't make it one bit easier to take.

When he'd left her in Paris, he'd left her abruptly. Not that he'd ever promised to stay. Not that he'd ever promised anything. But still . . .

He'd fallen asleep in the car the day she'd driven him back from Cannes. He'd awakened to discover that they were on the Corniche, half a mile from the twisting bend where the drunken driver in the red Peugeot had forced him off the road.

Poor Celeste. She hadn't known about the accident. And she sure as hell hadn't known what had hit her when Metrand had turned almost violently angry, starting a fight over something so stupid he couldn't even remember what it was. And he'd started packing when they'd entered the house.

Afterwards, he hadn't been able to explain, hadn't wanted to explain, hadn't wanted anything, except to heal his reopened wounds, to be alone and unattached to anyone. Later, when he thought it over carefully, he thought, *It's all for the best.* There was nothing he could give. And there was nothing he wanted badly enough to take on the burdens of loving another person to get it.

And so, he'd thought, it was just as well that he'd saved her from wasting any more of her time on a man and an adventure that was leading her nowhere. He'd conceded, at the time, that he'd behaved like a bastard, but he'd nonetheless done her a favor in the long run. Still, she was entitled to her piece of revenge. If he wanted her now, she was right to say no.

And he wanted her now, and she'd said no, and he couldn't sleep. *C'est la vie.*

And he *still* couldn't sleep.

There was a knock on his door.

He looked at his watch. Twelve forty-five. Was it possible?

No. It would be Patroni.

"Just a moment," he said, and walked to the door.

14.

Harrison stared at Halpern for a while, then looked at the glowing cigarette he was holding. "We live in fame or go down in flames," he mumbled. "But nothing can stop the Army Air Corps."

"Does that have a deep philosophical meaning? Or are you just singing old war songs to yourself?"

"It means, what time is the drone test tomorrow?"

"Six-thirty," Halpern said. "An hour after dawn."

"All things considered, I think we should delay it for a couple of hours, don't you?"

"Does *that* have a deeper meaning?"

"What kind of deeper meaning could it have?

Halpern stared at him, and nodded slowly. "If you say so," he said. "We'll delay it till . . . nine?"

Harrison nodded. "Delay and reprogram. Can you do it?"

"I guess."

"You guess?"

"I can."

Harrison stubbed his cigarette out. He picked up another. "Then do it," he said.

II

1.

"This is Robert Palmer at Gate Twenty-one at Dulles International Airport, where Concorde flight number one-seventeen is about to take off for Paris and Moscow. And waiting to board that special flight, we've got quite a collection of celebrities with us. These folks behind me in the red blazers are members of the Russian Olympic team. Gregori Yeshenko, flex a muscle for us."

Gregori stood up like a rising mountain; he grinned. "Well, that's a good muscle to flex," Palmer said quickly. "Gregori is the world's weightlifting champion. And here beside him—" Palmer looked down at a shy little girl with thick blonde braids, whose face was buried in Gregori's knee— "is, I'd guess, about forty-five pounds of daughter. You think you can lift her, Gregori?"

"I try," Gregori said and, grunting as though he could barely make it, he lifted the small, giggling child.

"What's her name?" Palmer said.

"Irina."

"Irina?" He held out the mike. "That's a pretty impressive papa you've got there. What do you think?"

Gregori, laughing, translated quickly. Irina watched him with big brown eyes and then made some rapid signs with her hands. Palmer sucked his breath in. The kid was deaf. But Gregori was laughing. "She say I am bear. Papa Bear, she call me. She is not so impressed. She has seen bigger bears in the Moscow Zoo."

"Well, we'll all be in Moscow on Monday morning," Palmer said smoothly. "And we'll see if she's right. Ah! And here's the gymnastic champion, Tatyana Rogov. Tanya?" He held out the mike and looked at her levelly. "How do you feel about leaving the States?" He paused. "About leaving the states forever?"

She stared at him, flushed, and ran a hand through the waves of her heavy dark hair. "It has been . . . a very pleasant vacation."

"But you're eager to return."

She hesitated. "Yes."

"I see. Then you must have a boyfriend in Moscow." *Jesus,* he thought. *Why am I doing this?* But he didn't stop doing it. "Do you?" he asked.

"I have," she said pointedly. "And a very large family I love very much. They . . . would suffer if I stay here longer. They would miss me," she added quickly, and smiled. "Now, if you'll excuse me—" And she moved past his elbow, and walked up to her coach.

The camera was running. Palmer looked at Arnie Kleber, who was behind it. Kleber shook his head and released the button. The camera stopped. Kleber scratched his beard. "*That* was nice," he muttered dryly. "What are you—?"

"Just run your camera, Arnie."

Kleber ran his camera.

"There's drama here too," Palmer said soberly. "That three-foot steel container you can see being wheeled by us is a thermal container, containing a heart. A human heart, being rushed on this plane to a Paris hospital, for a transplant that will save an eight-year-old boy. Uh, hold it. I think this gentleman here— You're Doctor Stone?"

The slight, balding surgeon nodded.

"You're going to perform this operation?"

"Yes."

"How long can the heart survive?"

"About five hours, under these conditions."

"So in other words, without the Concorde—"

"That's right. It wouldn't last through a conventional flight." He beetled his brows. "I hope nothing happens to delay this one. Though they say the Concorde flies above the weather and above the jet stream, so it isn't likely there'll be any delays."

"Thank you, Doctor." Palmer had to make an instant decision. Behind the doctor was Mrs. Gaminsky, the mother of the boy who'd be receiving the heart. A heartwarming story? Or the lighter-hearted note that would probably come from old Eli Sande?

"Mr. Sande?" Palmer said. "You're flying your own Concorde to Paris?"

"Depends what you mean by flying it." Sande was a crusty, handsome man in his middle seventies. "I'm flying *on* it." He laughed. "I'm leaving the piloting to less experienced hands."

"Less experienced?" Palmer asked.

"Listen, I've been flying planes since 1920. That's fifty-nine years. The captain? He's good. But he's only been flying for—what? Twenty, twenty-five years?"

Palmer laughed. "Well, that's good enough for me."

"Tell that to my wife." Sande jerked his head at a great-looking redhead of no more than thirty. "Amy? Come here."

She moved to the microphone, looked up quickly at the camera, and flushed.

"Are you nervous," Palmer asked, "about flying the Concorde?"

"Nope." Amy Sande was shaking her head. "I'm nervous about flying anything at all."

"With your husband the president of FWA, isn't that a little—"

"Awkward?" she interrupted him quickly. "Nope. What it is, is a *lot* awkward." She laughed.

Palmer pushed the microphone back at Sande. Sande was laughing.

"You don't seem to care too much," Palmer smiled, "if your wife tells a couple million people that she's scared of flying."

"Hell, no," Sande said. "I don't care what she says. As long as she doesn't blab that *I'm* scared of cats."

"Are you?"

"Hell, no," Sande said and walked off.

"He is," Amy whispered. And her husband pulled her away by the arm.

Palmer laughed. "I see some other celebrities here. Gretchen Carter, probably one of America's greatest jazz singers. She's on her way to perform a concert in Moscow. And there's Carla Thomas, the fourteen-year-old Olympic contender from Cranston, Minnesota. Let's see if we can talk to . . ."

"Federation World Airlines flight one-seventeen, for Paris and Moscow, has now begun boarding at Gate Twenty-one. Will passengers holding confirmed reservations . . ."

Maggie, in a phone booth across from the gate, drummed the receiver she held to her ear and loosened her jacket. She'd been left in the limbo of a long-distance hold, while a girl at a switchboard in Beverly Hills went hunting for the number of Jeffrey's room. The call was the tenth one Maggie had placed. She'd been trying to get hold of Jeffrey Marks since two in the morning. He'd been in transit till after midnight, but so far he hadn't checked into his room. It was now almost six A.M. in California.

Sighing, she glanced through the doors of the booth. Two feet in front of it, Detectives Dawson and Antonelli were standing like a couple of burly bookends. Their job was to see that she got safely on the plane, and whether she thought it was nonsense or not, she was stuck with them. Dawson shot her a glance. She tapped the receiver, shrugged, and then smiled. The detective shrugged back and turned. In the distance, Kleber was packing his camera, handing a film can to one of the crew. The film he'd just shot might or might not make the evening news, depending on how many earth-shaking stories broke between now and a quarter of six.

The operator said, "It's room twenty-three. Just a second. I'll ring." Another *click* into limbo again.

Maggie groaned. Her urgent call to the newsroom last night had yielded her nothing. The night man had checked over Jeffrey's office as well as Maggie's and Annabelle's. Zip. No envelope. Sorry. And with two policemen parked at her door and ready to follow wherever she went, going to the office herself was out.

The phone at the other end was ringing. "H'lo," Jeffrey said. He sounded asleep.

Maggie turned quickly, facing the wall. "Jeff, this is Maggie. I haven't much time, so wake up and listen. Annabelle gave you an envelope yesterday. My name was on it, and all of my notes—"

"I know. So?"

"You never gave it back to me."

"Jesus, I didn't think you'd need it, you know? I mean, the interview was over. It was yesterday's news."

"Or tomorrow's."

"Huh?"

"What did you do with it?"

"The envelope? What's all the—?"

"Jeffrey! Please!"

He yawned. "I dumped it on Annabelle's desk."

"And what did *she* do with it?"

"Annabelle? Christ. Probably mailed it to the IRS instead of her taxes."

"Jeffrey, don't joke."

He seemed to wake up. "Maggie, I really don't know where it is. I left it with Annabelle, that's all I know. Call her at home if you need it."

"I tried. She doesn't answer. Do you know the name of the guy she lives with?"

"Uh-uh. Maggie, what's this about? It sounds like it's—"

"Jeffrey, I have to go now. Forget I called you. Have a good trip."

"Yeah." He sounded confused. "You too."

She hung up the phone and looked at her watch. There was nothing to do. Annabelle wouldn't get to the office till ten. And that was too late. The best she could do now was phone in from Paris. She picked up her handbag and opened the booth.

Dawson and Antonelli looked up.

David was running toward her. The detectives started to block him.

"No!" Maggie shouted, and laughed. "He's a friend."

The policemen stopped, glowered, and watched as David embraced her.

"Sorry I'm late. The traffic—"

"You didn't have to bother," she said, kissing him again. "But I'm glad you did."

He pulled away and studied her, frowning. "Are you really okay?"

"I'm fine. Just exhausted."

"You'll sleep on the plane." Holding her hand, he started to walk her slowly to the gate. "I'll miss you," he said.

"I'll miss you too." She felt like a terrible traitor, still checking up on him. "Darling," she said, squeezing his hand. *Forgive me,* she added silently.

"What?"

"Nothing. Just 'darling.' "

"Oh." He smiled.

The detectives were keeping a discreet distance.

"Did those mysterious documents ever turn up?" he asked, laughing. "You know—the Parker Papers?"

"No," she said. "Why would they?"

He shrugged. "They wouldn't." He smiled. "I was making a joke."

They'd reached the final departure gate.

"Passengers only beyond this point." A steward examined her boarding pass. "Fine. This way, Miss Whelan."

"*This* way, Miss Whelan," David said, cupping her chin in his hand. He kissed her again. "Bon voyage," he whispered. "Take care of yourself. And of David Junior."

She clung to him for a moment, and finally pulled herself away. He turned, waving. She started through the gate.

"Hold it!" a woman's voice yelled behind her. "Maggie?"

She turned.

It was Annabelle Whitman, running, her springy ringlets bouncing on her head, a manila envelope clutched in her hand. She shouted again, "Maggie! Wait!"

Dawson turned. "This a friend of yours too?"

She nodded as Annabelle rushed up beside her.

David had turned; he watched her, and so did the two detectives.

"Maggie, these notes—" Annabelle panted. "They aren't—"

"*Thank* you," Maggie said quickly, cutting her off.

"I opened—"

"*Thank* you," Maggie said again, and turned before Annabelle could say another word.

Holding the envelope, she ran down the walkway and onto the plane.

2.

Stooping slightly in the five feet of headroom at the front of the cockpit, Metrand squeezed sideways into his seat. Patroni, flying as first officer, had already settled in the seat to his right. O'Neill, at the engineer's station behind him, was facing the board.

Patroni yawned. "Quite a night," he said.

Metrand shrugged. "Me, I was sound asleep by eleven."

"That so?" Patroni said. "Celeste and I didn't get back till midnight."

"That so?" Metrand said. He turned to O'Neill. "And how was *your* night? You still on that diet?"

O'Neill looked up. "Terrible, and yes, to answer your questions in order. I was almost seduced by a sirloin steak."

"But you're still a virgin?"

"Oh, yeah," O'Neill nodded. "I'll go home to my wife with a beautiful cholesterol-free conscience."

Metrand shook his head and looked at Patroni.

"Meatless diet," Metrand explained. "Saltless and coffeeless. And tasteless." He turned to O'Neill. "So what did you have?"

"A fruit compote and a sleepless night. I kept waking up from terrible dreams where I was being hounded by a vicious orange."

Patroni laughed, and then turned as Celeste said, "Coffee, Messieurs?"

"Double and black," Metrand said quickly.

Patroni laughed. "Those early nights really do a guy in." He looked at Celeste. "The captain had an exciting night, he tells me."

"Oh?" Celeste flushed and glared at Metrand. *"Saliguad,"* she said. *"Il faut déconner?"*

"Non. Je te jure."

"Toujours, tu jures!" Her voice was like ice.

"Celeste?"

"Au diable!" She turned and stalked out.

"Hey," Patroni said, "what did I—?" He frowned. "Did I put my foot in it?"

"No. Don't worry," Metrand said softly. "You put *my* foot in it."

"Oh, Jesus. I'm sorry. I didn't know. Really."

"But now you do."

Patroni nodded. "She's a wonderful girl. You're a lucky guy."

"Yeah," Metrand said.

"What did she say?"

"Just now? Nothing much. She called me a louse. And a bigmouth. And told me to go to hell. That's all."

"Oh." Patroni winced. "Maybe—" He started to get up.

"Sit down." Metrand jerked his thumb at the clock on the console. "Time to go to work."

O'Neill read the checklist. Metrand and Patroni tested the switches, checked the controls.

"Ramp?"

108

"Open."

"Spill doors?"

"Closed."

"Coffee."

Metrand looked up at Celeste. Without expression, she handed him the cup. "Celeste?" he said.

She turned quickly and left.

Patroni looked at him.

"Mind your own business."

Patroni said, "Check."

"Mind a few visitors?" a voice said behind them. Eli Sande came in with his wife. "How are you, Joe? Captain?" He nodded quickly at Metrand. "I'd like you to meet my, uh, 'old lady.'" He laughed. "I want you to tell her there's nothing to worry about."

"Safer than taking a bus," Metrand said.

Sande laughed. "She's afraid of buses."

"It's safer than walking," Metrand tried again.

Amy nodded. "Okay, but is it safer than staying at home?"

"Sure," Metrand laughed. "More pilots slip in their bathtubs than slip in their cockpits. Listen, Mrs. Sande. This plane can come home with four engines out."

"How many engines does it have?"

"Four."

"Oh, Lord," Amy said.

Sande shook his head. "You gave her something else to worry about. Now tell her what it would take to make all four engines go out."

Metrand looked up. "World War Three."

"Feel better?" Sande asked her.

"Maybe," she said. "What are you doing?" She looked at Metrand, who was punching buttons on a boxy pedestal between his and the copilot's seat.

"This is Jacques," he said. "Our navigator." He presented the pedestal. "Meet Mrs. Sande. Inertial navigation system," he explained. "I'm punching in the longitudes and latitudes of Dulles Airport and all the checkpoints along the way."

"Jacques'll make sure we stay on our course," Patroni explained. "And then Al—the autopilot—he flies the plane."

"So what do you fellows do?" Amy asked.

"Us?" O'Neill said. "We play poker."

"You're kidding!"

"Sure," Patroni assured her. "Listen, what we *really* do is sit and get drunk."

"I think that's what Amy better do," Sande said with a chuckle. Metrand was strapping on his shoulder harness. "That's a hint," Sande said, "that we ought to take our seats."

"And relax," Metrand added. "I assure you, madame, you're in for the smoothest ride of your life."

Turning, he looked at the console before him. A blinking red light told him the fuselage door was still open; the boarding walkway was still attached. Either a VIP was late and the plane was being held, or a passenger had discovered he'd just lost his wallet and had run back to scour the waiting room floor.

Either way, he couldn't start the portside engines. They just had to sit here and wait.

3.

Harrison looked out the car window. They were driving the Potomac Parkway. The river was shimmering in the sun. "Beautiful day," he said to Halpern. They were the first words he'd spoken this morning. Sighing, he turned.

"Well?" Halpern said. Halpern looked tired. There were dark rings around his pale blue eyes. His beautifully barbered silver-gray hair was tousled; he'd been running his fingers through it.

Harrison shrugged. He glanced at the back of his chauffeur's neck through the green-tinted glass partition. "I don't know," he said slowly. "I really don't know."

"You better make up your mind." Halpern looked at his watch. It was seven minutes before nine.

"She seems all right, but just as she was leaving, a girl ran up and handed her some papers."

"*The* papers?"

"Christ, I don't know. It was a big envelope. The logo of the television station was on it. It could just have been notes for her trip."

Halpern looked thoughtful, then he whistled. "That's it. That's how he did it."

"How who did what?"

"Parker. How he got the papers out. I looked at the pictures—you know, the ones we take at the guard post at the door. That reporter, the one from 'On The Spot News'? He was holding one of those envelopes."

"So? He works for the same station. I know where you're leading, but—"

"It might mean the guy's involved in it too, as well as your Maggie."

"It might."

"Hey, look, this was your idea. If you want to change your mind, you've got seven minutes. Correction. You've now got six and a half."

The phone on the armrest was ringing. Harrison pounced on it.

"David?" Maggie stood in the waiting room phone booth.

"Maggie? How did—"

"I got off the plane. They're holding it for me. I said it was urgent. It *is* urgent, David. I have the documents. Some of them I don't completely understand, but I understand the ones that prove you're the owner of Armuco Munitions."

"Maggie, I—"

"No. Don't lie to me, David. You lied to me before when you said you didn't own it. You do. And the papers show—"

"Maggie, will you—?"

"No. You had Parker killed, didn't you, David?"

"No! My God. Will you listen to me, Maggie?

112

I've—I've done a lot of things I regret, but I'm not a killer."

"Just a traitor, huh?"

"Not a traitor either. Honey, there are things you don't understand. Those documents—they affect a lot of people. A lot of . . . a lot of deadly men."

"And you're not one of them? You just sell the guns but you don't pull the triggers? Does that make you clean?"

"Maggie, you don't understand this, believe me. But you know me. You know I'm not a violent man."

She looked out through the glass doors of the booth. People were passing with golf clubs and bags, laughing. A couple kissed at the gate. And she did know David. As a tender man. As her lover. As the father of her child. "I'm not—I'm not sure I know anything about you. David? I have to warn you, when I hang up, I'm calling a friend at the CIA."

"Maggie, you can't!" He sounded in agony.

She steeled herself. "The dimes in my hand say I can. He'll understand the papers and also the blueprints. If you're innocent, David, you can trust him. He's—"

"Swell. And how about you trusting me? My God, after all this time. You're having my child. If you trust me or love me at all, just hold those papers. I'll meet you in Paris. You're staying at the Ritz, aren't you? Wait for me there and just let me explain."

"I . . ." The tears were starting now. "I can't."

"Then you don't love me."

"The saddest damn part of it is that I do. I still love you, David. I—" She could see the stewardess, moving through the gate, looking for her.

"Well . . . it's up to you, Maggie."

She gulped back the tears and rubbed her eyes. "I'll . . . I'll see you in Paris," she said.

Harrison hung up and turned to Halpern. "She's got them," he said. "Papers and blueprints."

"We proceed?"

"We proceed."

The car made a turn through the airfield gates. The chauffeur showed his pass to the Harrison guard, who leaned over quickly and peered through the window. Seeing who it was, he smiled and made a fast, friendly salute.

They drove past the Dragonfly, waiting on its stand.

"You programmed it?" Harrison asked.

"Last night. There's no way anyone'll ever find out. Not even the men up in Mission Control. When they see where it's heading, they'll sit there punching all the right buttons, but the buttons won't work. After I give it the final instructions, the drone won't respond to any interference. It'll look like an accident, some kind of quirky mechanical failure."

Harrison buried his face in his hands. "Just when we were proving how perfect it is. Christ. What a lousy trade-off, Bill. It's gonna set us back."

"Not as far back as those documents would."

The limousine pulled up in front of the tower.

Harrison sat without moving for a moment. "I know," he said, nodding slowly. He opened the door. "Come on. Let's go."

4.

The blinking light on the console went dark, indicating that the fuselage door had been closed. The boarding walkway was being removed. The interphone crackled, "Okay to start."

Metrand acknowledged. He reached for the start levers under the throttles and, one by one, fired the powerful Olympus engines. They caught and held with a resonant whine.

"FWA flight one-one-seven from ground control. You're cleared to taxi."

The engines quickened, and the Concorde began its ride down the road.

In the cabin, Celeste turned on the intercom. "Ladies and gentlemen, Captain Metrand and the rest of the crew wish to welcome you aboard flight one-seventeen for Paris and Moscow. Our estimated flying time is three hours and fifty minutes. We'll arrive in Paris at De Gaulle Airport at five fifty-two P.M., local time. The weather in Paris . . ."

* * *

"There's also an American embassy in Paris," Palmer whispered in Tatyana's ear.

She turned and looked him directly in the eye. "There's also a Russian embassy in Paris. Why don't *you* defect? You'd make a good Russian."

"No, I wouldn't. I'd wind up in jail in twenty-five minutes. I'm too independent. I don't want to be a Russian."

"Fine. I don't want to be an American either."

"Okay. We could take an apartment in Paris. Or Stockholm. Tanya, I'd even live in Iceland. I just want to marry you."

Her eyes were misty when she looked at him again. "To Americans," she said, "life is so simple."

"Life isn't simple for anyone, Tanya. But you're right. It's simpler for Americans than for most. Marry me," he whispered, and kissed her.

She pushed him away, shaking her head, looking out the window. "Marriage is very complicated, Robert. For anyone. And very much more so for us."

Palmer gave a weary sigh. He looked up slowly. Standing beside him, in the aisle on his left, was Nelli, Tanya's gymnastic coach. Nelli was a tough, wiry old bird. At fifty, she could probably bend over backwards and touch the floor. And that, he thought wryly, was probably all she'd ever touched. She looked like the ultimate dried-up old maid.

"Change seats with me, Tanya," she ordered crisply.

"She can't," Palmer said.

"She can and she will. She is under my—"

"Thumb," Palmer said, finishing the sentence. "But she's also under FAA regulations. She can't change seats till the belt sign is off." He gestured toward the FASTEN SEAT BELTS sign.

A stewardess moved up to Nelli. "Madame? You'll have to—"

"All right!" Nelli said brusquely. She looked at Palmer. "But I will be back."

She moved down the aisle, taking her seat as the intercom spoke:

"This is Captain Metrand. We're waiting in line on the runway now. There's one plane ahead of us and then we'll go. We'll be climbing to an altitude of fifty-nine thousand feet and cruising at an airspeed of Mach two. That's thirteen hundred and fifty miles an hour, and for all you Superman fans, that's literally faster than a speeding bullet. You can watch our speed on the cabin Machmeter—that's the digital speedometer at the front of the cabin. When it hits Mach one, that's the speed of sound. If you wonder how you'll feel moving faster than sound, you won't feel any difference at all. The only thing different about flying at supersonic speed is that the flight will be smoother, and of course a lot shorter. We hope you'll enjoy it."

He clicked off the intercom, cleared his throat, and waited for the signal from the ground controller. It came: "Cleared for takeoff."

With a steady motion, he pushed the throttles to full thrust, and the plane began to move.

It picked up speed quickly.

"A hundred knots," Patroni reported.

Metrand flicked his eyes to the console. A hundred and thirty knots.

"V-one," Patroni said.

Metrand nodded. The V-one speed—the ratio of aircraft weight and momentum to the length of the runway—was also known as "decision speed." Once you exceeded it, you had to take off, because you'd run out of runway before you could brake.

"Rotate."

Metrand eased back on the controls, lifting the nose.

Airborne.

The plane started its steep-angled climb.

In Mission Control at Harrison Aircraft, Anson McGuire looked at the screen. Across from him, Spannell monitored communications from Dulles.

"FWA flight one-one-seven from Dulles Tower. Turn left. Cleared to flight level five-nine-zero."

On the radar, McGuire was tracking the left turn of the Concorde. Beside him, Parkinson reached for the microphone and spoke into it: "Dulles Tower from Harrison Mission Control. Keeping you advised. Dragonfly test flight starts in five minutes."

"Roger, Harrison," Dulles came back. "Keep monitoring our traffic and keep us informed."

Harrison and Halpern had entered the room.

"One-one-seven from Dulles Tower. Cleared to climb to twenty-five thousand."

"Roger, Dulles." Patroni leaned back, his eyes on the instruments. The flight director, a piece of equipment unique to the Concorde, computed the ideal path of ascent. Aside from that, the controls and the instrument panels were conventional, similar to any subsonic craft. Patroni felt at home. He'd been carefully trained, and by the time he completed this round trip to Dulles under Metrand's supervision, he'd be fully qualified to pilot a Concorde. He turned to Metrand. "You flew supersonic in the Air Force, I hear."

"*L'Armée de l'Air,* we call it. Yes. I flew the Mirage."

Patroni nodded. "I used to fly the F-4E, the 14A, and the 104. On the other hand, I've also flown a B-29."

Metrand looked at him.

Patroni shrugged. "I've fought in three wars." He

grinned. "The only thing I'm afraid of is heights. How about you? Are you afraid of anything?"

"Yes," Metrand said. "American pilots."

Harrison was watching the field through binoculars. Halpern stood at McGuire's shoulder.

"Target plane airborne," Handler reported.

McGuire tracked its blip on the radar in front of him.

"Dragonfly operative," Handler said. "Cameras operative. On-board computer operative." The final countdown began. "Ignition."

The drone took off.

On Spannell's radio, tuned into Dulles communications, a voice said, "Concorde one-one-seven. Turn right on a heading of zero-three-five."

Halpern moved away.

Out of the corner of an eye still fixed on the face of the radar screen, McGuire saw Halpern head for the computer.

Two seconds later, hell—or, rather, the Harrison Dragonfly—broke loose.

"Drone off course," McGuire reported.

The Dragonfly had suddenly veered to the left.

"Stand by for termination," Handler said.

On Spannell's radio, the Dulles frequency crackled: "One-one-seven. Northbound traffic at three o'clock. Slow-moving."

"Roger. Thank you, Dulles," came the Concorde's reply.

Behind McGuire, Handler said urgently, "Dragonfly not responding to commands."

On the scope now, the drone continued to move; no longer in pursuit of the unmanned target, it arced to the left.

"What's going on?" David Harrison had moved from the window.

"Malfunction," Handler said.

"Terminate it."

"Tried. The terminator switch doesn't seem to respond."

"Bring it back then," Harrison snapped.

"Mach one," the Concorde reported to Dulles.

McGuire, his eyes on the radar, listened:

"Air France twenty, this is Washington Center. We just had a blip at three-six-zero and we lost it. Do you have any visual contact with a fast-moving northbound UFO?"

"Negative, Washington. A 747 at six o'clock, and the Concorde went by at altitude."

"Roger. Concorde one-one-seven, can you see any unknown traffic at four o'clock?"

"Negative, Washington. We have a 747 at four o'clock and a 727 at nine-thirty. What's the problem?"

"No problem, Concorde. We've just got an intermittent contact. Will identify."

McGuire knew what that contact was. The unidentified flying object wasn't unidentified at all. It was the Harrison Dragonfly. There was still time to stop it, to turn it around. Or maybe there wasn't.

"It's not responding to radio control," Handler announced.

Halpern looked up. "Computer malfunction. What's its course?"

McGuire said quickly, "Zero-three-five. The exact heading of the Dulles eastbound. We've got to—"

"Tell Washington Center. Fast," Harrison exploded at Spannell.

"Yes, sir. Washington Center, this is Harrison Aircraft Mission Control. Emergency. Dragonfly out of control. Set on a heading of zero-three-five, airspeed Mach two."

"Bill, try again," Harrison ordered. "See if you can get that computer to respond."

"I'm trying," Halpern said. "Nothing. The damn thing's got a mind of its own."

"To all aircraft from Dulles Tower. Maintain present altitudes and vector spaces. Emergency. Repeat, emergency. We've got a malfunctioning drone in the sky, heading zero-three-five. The Air Force is responding."

"The Air Force?" Harrison looked at Halpern, who turned to Spannell. "Monitor Langley Air Force Base."

"Monitor Langley," Patroni said.

The radio spoke again: "Concorde, we lost the Dragonfly again. The sonofabitch is too damn small. It might have changed headings; we just don't know. Stand by."

"Better warn the passengers, Joe."

"Me?" Patroni looked up at Metrand. "You're the captain."

"Officially, yes. But an American voice will sound more reassuring."

"To the Russians?"

Metrand gave a quick, dry laugh. "Just keep your tone light."

"I know how to keep it." Patroni reached for the intercom and practically yawned, "Hi. Sorry to bother you folks, but Washington Center has just advised that we might have to make a few changes in course. So we'd like you to stay in your seats for a while, with your seat belts fastened. I'm, uh, going to turn on some music in the cabin, but, uh, please refrain from dancing in the aisles."

O'Neill looked at him. "That's the Olympic Airways slogan."

"Yeah? Let 'em sue me," Patroni said.

"Four o'clock, Captain!" O'Neill said crisply. Metrand saw the Dragonfly as it aimed for the Concorde's belly.

He maneuvered the plane in a radical bank. The Dragonfly missed them, but not by much, and went blasting off into the blue.

Patroni whistled. "Where the hell did it go?" He and Metrand squinted through the window. Nothing.

"Maybe we should change our course. The tower can't help us; they can't see it either." Metrand was frowning.

Patroni shook his head. "Those drones lock on with a guidance system. If we juke around the sky, it'll only nail us when we can't even see it. Better let the bastard make the first move. When we know what it's doing, then we'll react."

O'Neill, at the radio, reported quickly, "Langley's sending some F-15s."

"F-15s moving from Langley," Spannell reported.

On the monitor, the relayed television pictures being taken by the Dragonfly flashed on the screen.

"It's locked on the Concorde," Harrison said.

Somebody whistled. "What a maneuver! That Concorde pilot—look at him go!"

The Concorde had taken another steep dive.

"I wouldn't want to be in that passenger cabin," Spannell said. "Man! They gotta be bouncing around like Mexican jumping beans."

"I wouldn't want to be in that Concorde at all," McGuire said softly.

The Dragonfly missed the airliner again, but the Concorde couldn't duck fate forever.

And the planes from Langley were too far away.

The Dragonfly turned, heading once more for the weaving Concorde.

"F-15s at ten o'clock," Metrand said tersely.

Wing to wing, the Air Force fighters screamed toward the drone. Metrand knew the F-15s had been built to combat the MIG-23, and ought to be able to take on a drone. *As long as the drone's fixed on us,* he thought. *And as long as it's—*

The drone made another pass.

"Roll!" Patroni yelled, and they banked, rolled over, leveled, and the drone came at them again.

"Can't shake the bastard!"

"She's coming at our nose!"

"She's dead," Halpern said grimly. "She's a goner."

Again, the pictures from the Dragonfly's nose showed the nimble maneuvers of the captive Concorde.

The radio frequency from Langley came to life: "Drone in sight. Arming air-to-air . . ."

Harrison stood at McGuire's radarscreen. "Fighters are too close now. If they overshoot, the Concorde will wind up with a missile in its lap."

"Firing one," the Air Force reported.

The Dragonfly's cameras went black.

And its dot on McGuire's scope disappeared.

"Thank God," McGuire said.

"Dragonfly terminated," Handler announced.

McGuire looked at Harrison.

Harrison turned and walked out of the room.

5.

Eli Sande walked into the cockpit. "What in God's name was *that* all about?"

Patroni explained.

"Well, you better get on that microphone and tell them."

"Can't," Metrand said.

"What's that supposed to mean?" Sande narrowed his eyes. "You've got ninety-one terrified people back there."

"Any other damage?"

"A lot of blankets dropped from the racks. A lot of hand luggage rolled out from under the seats. I don't know if anybody's hurt or not, but don't change the subject. Why can't you tell them?"

"We can tell them something, but not the truth. The Air Force wants us to shut up about it until they investigate."

"So what will you say we were dodging out there?"

"I don't know," Metrand said.

"A flying saucer?" O'Neill suggested.

Patroni looked at him. "That'll keep 'em calm," he said sarcastically. He turned to Sande. "Could you see the F-15s through the window?"

"Sure as hell could."

Patroni nodded and reached for the mike as Celeste walked in.

"Nobody seems to be injured," she said, "but there's a doctor on board—a Dr. Stone. He's volunteered his services if anyone—"

Metrand cut her off. "Fine. Joe, I think you and Celeste should go out to the cabin. Tell them—whatever you think might calm them down. Better they should see a human being than just hear a voice."

Patroni nodded and gestured to Celeste. "Come with me," he said. "Two phony smiles are better than one."

They walked silently down the center aisle. Quickly and carefully, Patroni made mental notes of the damage. There was debris in the aisle from a few dozen open cosmetics cases. The air reeked with perfume, spilled on the carpet. Which was not entirely a terrible thing, since a couple of people had lost their breakfasts and, unhappily, found them again on their laps. Considering that the plane had turned upside down a couple of times, the damage was minimal. A bearded man with aviator glasses was filming the scene with a television camera.

Smiling, Patroni reached for the intercom phone. The television camera focused on his smile.

"Let me begin," Patroni said slowly, "by saying we have a doctor on board, so if anybody here needs medical attention, just give your name to the flight attendant. I'd like to assure you we've run a complete check on the plane and everything checks out in perfect order." He paused, looked around at the troubled faces. "I know," he said, "that it must have felt like a century or so, but we only lost seven minutes back there, and we'll continue to Paris on course and on time—plus seven minutes." He looked around, smiling. Celeste was smiling. Maybe, he thought, he could just quit now, turn around, smiling, and walk up the aisle.

Wrong.

"Exactly what happened, Captain?"

Patroni turned. The question had come from a doll of a blonde, and the face and the voice rang a silvery bell in his memory. Maggie Whelan. He'd met her before, at the Salt Lake City airport in '75, when a wounded 747 came down. And he'd seen her news show in Washington. Caution: reporter, he thought. He took a deep breath, and exhaled it through his smile. "Well, I can't tell you exactly, Miss Whelan. I don't *know* exactly. But, uh, some fighters from Langley got off their course and we had to make adjustments to avoid a collision."

"Oh." She nodded. "Those were some 'adjustments.' "

"Yeah," Patroni said. "Well, if that's all, the war's over now. Relax. And you could probably all use a drink."

There seemed to be general agreement on that.

Celeste said quietly, "Nice work, Joe," and then, louder, "We'll be taking your orders for drinks." Patroni continued up the aisle, heading for the relative safety of the flight deck.

A hand reached out and tugged at his sleeve. Another reporter: Robert Palmer.

"Well, hi, there," Patroni said, and tried unobtrusively to get his sleeve back.

"Sorry," Palmer said. "I just want to know what's up it."

"My sleeve?"

"Exactly."

126

"Nothing."

"Then why the bullshit?"

"What bullshit?" Patroni asked.

"You weren't dodging any F-15s. Not if they were manned by the Air Force, you weren't." Palmer looked Patroni in the eye.

"Who else would have F-15s?" Patroni asked.

"Terrorists?"

"Are you asking me or telling me, Palmer?"

"I don't know."

"Well, neither do I. And I think you better keep your speculations to yourself. When you get to Paris, you can check with the Air Force."

"Don't think I won't."

"I don't," Patroni said, and continued to the flight deck.

Palmer watched him go. It didn't make sense. The F-15's had flown at the Concorde in combat formation. One of them had fired some missiles. It had to have been a terror attack. And yet— How did terrorists commandeer a couple of armed F-15s—over U.S. waters? If that was the story, it had to be the biggest story of the year. Or the decade.

Palmer turned around and looked at Tatyana. She was having a hot discussion with Nelli. Probably about double sommersaults. The only subject on Nelli's mind. Turning again, Palmer shook his head.

Tatyana closed her eyes.

Nelli was saying, "Your performance yesterday was very clumsy. You weren't concentrating."

Tatyana said nothing. A moment ago, it had looked as though they might be diving into death, and Nelli was now discussing her performance. The advantages of a one-track mind. Tatyana wasn't blessed with a one-track mind. And she *hadn't* been concentrating yesterday morning. She'd been thinking of Robert.

"I—I understand what you're going through, Tanya," Nelli said suddenly.

Tatyana sat up, opening her eyes. Nelli was watching her as though she really *might* understand.

Nelli smiled. "You think that's impossible? At the Olympics in Rome, I met a swimmer from Holland. He asked me to marry him."

"And why—why didn't you?"

Nelli looked away. "I was young . . . and afraid."

"Are you sorry now that you didn't marry him?"

Nelli didn't answer. She stared out the window. They were flying through clouds. "No," she said finally. "No. Of course not."

Celeste stopped at their seats. "Would either of you like a drink?" she asked. "Or a soft drink? Coffee?"

The women shook their heads, and Celeste moved on.

Dr. Stone, the surgeon, was moving down the aisle. "I've just checked the heart," he said to her. "It's all right. The container wasn't jostled and there's plenty of ice." He smiled dryly. "Those 'adjustments' were enough to stop anyone's heart."

"Well, it's all over now."

"I just hope we won't be losing more time. After we land, I've only got an hour to get to the hospital. Those seven minutes we lost—"

"Don't worry," Celeste said quickly. "There's no reason now for us to lose more time."

"I hope not." The doctor moved to his seat.

"Do you really think they were terrorists?" a voice said behind her.

"Keep it quiet, Maggie."

Celeste turned around. Maggie Whelan and Robert Palmer were whispering.

She asked them if they wanted a drink.

*   *   *

David Harrison poured himself a drink and reached for the phone. He dialed the code numbers: 011—for Europe; 33—for France; 1—for Paris; and then the number for Andre Robelle's private office on the Rue Vaugirard. He waited impatiently, drumming on his desk and sipping his whiskey, till the phone at the other end was answered with Robelle's sharp and strident, *"J'écoute."*

"Andre? It's David. In Washington."

"Ah. And how is the weather in Washington?"

"Hot."

"I see."

"How's the weather in Paris?"

"Pleasant. Quite pleasant."

"The forecast says it might get stormy."

There was a pause, then Robelle said slowly, "Go on."

"I have a friend arriving on a Concorde today. Flight one-seventeen from Washington."

"What time does it arrive?"

Harrison finished his drink and poured another. "The prediction of storms made me wonder if the plane would arrive at all."

Another pause. "Of course, anything's possible. On the other hand—" Robelle hesitated—"would it not be simpler if we simply met your friend at the airport?"

Harrison paused, searching for the right unincriminating words that would still make his point. "That's a kind offer, Andre. Perhaps too kind. Her American uncle may meet her at the airport, but in any case—" Again, he searched for the words. The point was that any violent action aimed specifically at Maggie Whelan would, after last night's attack on Parker, lead to suspicions of a Harrison link. "I would simply suggest that the uncle would be vastly impressed with such a gesture."

"J'y suis. I get it. You don't want her uncle to

know that the two of you . . ." Robelle laughed suggestively.

"Exactly." Harrison laughed in relief. Robelle had managed to give it the sound of romantic liaison, disapproved of by an uncle. "In any case, I'm flying to Paris myself. I can . . . arrange for a private rendezvous."

"Ah."

"If all else fails."

"It won't," Robelle said.

"We'll talk in Paris."

"D'accord. Au revoir."

"A bientôt."

Harrison hung up the phone; he rubbed his jaw and then finished his drink. He would get very drunk on the flight to Paris. He did not want to think about what he was doing. He did not want to think about anything at all.

He buzzed for his secretary. "Get my plane ready. I'm flying to—" he hesitated, calculating an equivalent in miles to be sure his plane would have the right amount of fuel. "To Rio," he said. "I'd like to leave within the hour."

6.

It was a bad day, and it was only twelve minutes old. It was twelve after ten, and it was raining again. McKeever had awakened hung over with exhaustion, feeling all the worse for his two and a half hours' sleep. He'd already managed to stub his toe and cut himself shaving, while the coffee in the kitchen boiled over on the stove. And before he'd even had a sip of what was left, Hamilton had called, saying, "Get your ass in here, McKeever. On the double."

On the double? *Nobody* said, "on the double" anymore. No living person had said "on the double" since they stopped doing re-runs of "Gomer Pyle."

McKeever got dressed. Hamilton was pissed. And to hell with him. McKeever's knee had an ache that four hundred aspirin wouldn't impress. His knee would just watch them charging through his bloodstream, yawn, and continue aching like hell. He'd injured it, climbing on Maggie's roof; it had buckled, scaring him. It wasn't as strong as he'd thought. The Case of the Weak-Kneed Spy. McKeever cursed and pulled on his jeans. Roger Hamilton cared about grooming almost as much as he cared about money, manners, background, and old school ties. The jeans would bug him. McKeever considered a yellow sweatshirt with *J'en ai soupé* written on its chest, but Hamilton wouldn't understand what it meant: *I'm fed up with this, buddy. I've had it up to here.* McKeever selected a turtleneck sweater with a hole in it. That ought to do just as well.

He strapped on his holster, threw on a raincoat, and raced around the corner in battering rain to the spot where he'd parked his beat-up MG.

There was a ticket on the windshield.

"Why wasn't I informed?" Hamilton said, "let alone consulted for approval?"

"You were . . . sir." McKeever put a slight emphasis on the "sir." "I filed a report. It's sitting on your desk."

"Yes. Seven hours after the fact. You realize the expenses you've authorized here?"

"I haven't authorized anything, sir. The point is, it's five hours later in Paris."

"So?"

"I had to call them in the middle of the night or I would have blown the whole thing. You can countermand the order."

"I want to know why you issued it in the first place." Hamilton reached for a folder on his desk and consulted a page of McKeever's report. "Round-the-clock protection for one Margaret Whelan." He looked up again. "You want her watched and protected without her awareness."

"She'll only be in Paris for twenty-two hours. I think we can afford—"

"Yes. But why should we? Because you've got a hunch? Because a little birdie whispered in your ear? We don't operate that way, McKeever."

And that, McKeever thought, is half of what's wrong with the way you *do* operate. Computerized gambits, directed on the path of highest probabilities, while life continues in its improbable course.

"There are elements of hunch." McKeever tried to keep the impatience from his voice. "But there are also some facts. Fact: the assassin Miss Whelan described fits the description of Anthony Cooper. Tall, clean, good-looking blond, expensively dressed in Paris-made clothes. Cooper's a hitman for Andre Robelle. Robelle had connections with Marc Dauphin. And Dauphin had connections to a gun ring we found and busted in Reims. But the whole thing goes a lot deeper than that."

"*What* thing goes a lot deeper than *what?*"

"Someplace in France, there's a central depot supplying terrorists with ammunition. And I think Dauphin and Robelle are behind it."

Hamilton nodded. It was a neutral gesture, meant to convey neither agreement nor acceptance. "And you've forged this link from Whelan to Robelle to the jackpot on the other side of the rainbow from a loose description she gave of a killer?"

"There's more," McKeever said. He was getting bored—fed up with explaining himself, and everything else, to a deskbound clunk. If he were back in Paris, reporting to Pearson, he could say two words and Pearson would nod, grin, say, "Gotcha," and that would be that. McKeever was dying to get up and pace, but with his knee sending waves of pain through his leg, he might start to limp. And that could be worth another seventeen years at a Washington desk. He lit a cigarette and looked up at

Hamilton's soft, pink face. "Whelan knows more than she's saying she knows."

"That's just another guess."

"An *educated* guess. I know the lady—well. She's holding out, protecting someone. Question: who? Answer: her lover. Question: who's he? Answer: David Harrison. Question: who's he? Answer:—"

"I know what the answer is, thanks."

"Mmm. You also know he owns Armuco Munitions, Trans-Europe Shipping, and—"

"What are you saying?"

"I'm saying it might make a nice, tight ball."

"If you think she knows something, you should have kept her here."

"Wrong. She wouldn't tell us and she'd also be in danger."

"We'd have given her protection."

"Yeah, sure. Her and Jack Kennedy."

"So what makes you think she'd be safer in Paris?"

"Letting her go could signal that we don't think she knows a damn thing. Which might make her safer, as long as she's protected by the Paris station. And after that, she's going to the safest place there is."

"Moscow?"

McKeever rolled his eyes to the ceiling. "It takes six weeks to get a visa to Russia. Four days, at least, to get a decent forgery, and the odds against its working are a million to one. So no one's gonna follow her in there to waste her. Not to mention that she'll be watched by the KGB, just for being an American journalist."

"Mmm." Hamilton nodded, slowly this time, like an idiot staring at a picture of a duck, labeled "DUCK," who'd just put it all together: Duck. "So, if we protect her and watch her in Paris, if someone tries to contact her there, we'll know."

"Uh-huh," McKeever said.

"Aha. So you think she's involved in it."

"No."

"No? But if she's—"

"No," McKeever said again. "I told you. I know her. I think she's being conned."

Hamilton cocked his head now and frowned. "Can you explain why you think that?"

"No."

Silence. Then Hamilton said quietly, "Just another *hunch,* McKeever?"

"Uh-huh." He suddenly laughed out loud.

"What's so funny?" Hamilton said.

McKeever shook his head. What was funny was McKeever—McKeever, with his ass and his job on the line for a girl he hadn't seen in a few million years, who hadn't loved him then, who wouldn't love him now, and who was furthermore in love with a brilliant, handsome, slick millionaire who was probably innocent of any of the crimes McKeever had been wishing on him all through the night.

"Nothing," McKeever said. "What's the verdict? Do we keep the surveillance in Paris, or what?"

Hamilton sighed and nodded. "I guess."

"Is that all, then?"

"Yes. Go home."

"Good. I could use a little sleep."

"I meant go home," Hamilton said, "put on some decent, respectable clothes, and be back for a meeting in forty-five minutes."

McKeever stood. "Yes . . . sir," he said.

7.

Celeste returned to the flight deck with a lunch tray
for Metrand. According to company regulations, Patroni would be given a different meal at a later time,
so that if, by some chance, the food was tainted, the
pilot and copilot wouldn't both get sick.

O'Neill eyed the tray. "Steak," he said. "You had
to have steak?"

"I'm not married," Metrand said quickly, "to
your wife."

"One of the pleasures of the bachelor life. Eating
what you want to," Patroni said, grinning. He suddenly sighed. "The only pleasure," he added, "for
me."

"I thought you were married. Didn't you mention
your wife last night?"

"Probably. I talk about her often, I guess. But
she's dead. Two years ago. Cancer. It was sudden
and very . . . brutal." Patroni shook his head. "And

136

my son's in college. How about some coffee, Celeste?"

"Of course."

Metrand started eating from the tray on his lap.

As she turned, Celeste put a hand on his shoulder. "You're quite a pilot, Captain," she said. She said it softly. Metrand looked up. She was smiling.

"I'm not still a louse?" he asked.

"Oh, you're still a louse." Her smile broadened. "But you're also an amazingly talented pilot. Those maneuvers—*terrible*."

Patroni frowned. "Terrible?"

"Terrific," Celeste translated. She turned to O'Neill. "And what would you like?"

"A steak and some coffee."

"Fine." She nodded and started to leave.

"But what I'll *have*," he said dully, "is a salad and milk." He swiveled in his chair and looked at Metrand. "And you really *are* a hell of a pilot."

"He's after your steak," Patroni said.

"You want to take over the rest of the flight?"

"You mean now that the hard part's over with?"

"Right," Metrand laughed. "You've flown more combat than I have, Joe. You'd have done just as well. Probably better."

"Hey, listen," O'Neill interrupted. "Paul? Now that it's over, I want to tell you about something eerie. I told you I had dinner with LeBec last night? Well, I not only watched him eat a sirloin steak, but I also watched him drink a lot of Beaujolais. And four glasses into it, he said he'd had a vision. Combat in the air, he said. An explosion. Terrorists, he said. And we'd lose control and dive into the sea."

"California Beaujolais." Metrand shook his head. "It'll do that every time."

"Well, he wasn't far wrong," O'Neill rebutted.

"He missed by a mile. No explosion, and we

didn't dive. But I'm glad you didn't share that prediction with us before," Metrand said slowly.

Celeste came back with a large bowl of salad, a glass of milk, and Eli Sande.

"You want to hear something incredible?" Sande said. "My wife—she slept through the whole damn thing. She's still asleep. Mind if I join you?"

"Make yourself at home."

"In one of these things? I'd be more at home in a biplane. Ha! I used to barnstorm in one of those things. A Spad. The best damn plane in the world."

"A French plane, you'll notice," Metrand said dryly.

"Damn right it was," Sande admitted quickly. "The French owned the air in the First World War. The Spad, the Nieuport. They had all the planes and they had all the pilots. Sure. The French taught us how to fly."

"The Lafayette Escadrille," Patroni said, turning to face Sande. "Is that where you trained?"

Sande raised his eyebrows. "Captain, I'm only seventy-three. In order to have trained in the Escadrille, I'd have to be at least eighty-one, eighty-two. That may not seem like a difference to you, but just you wait till *you're* seventy-three. No. I had a brother in the Escadrille, though. Trained in France. Flew at Verdun. Went down in a dogfight. You know what the life expectancy was, of a combat pilot in World War One? Three weeks. That was it. That's all it was. Things have improved a little since then."

"I don't know," Metrand said. "If they keep on 'improving' all those heat-seeking missiles and lasers, you'd be lucky to survive for an hour and a half."

"Well," Patroni said, stretching his arms, "in an hour and a half, we'll be landing in Paris." He gazed out the window and clicked on the mike.

"Ladies and gentlemen," Patroni announced, "we're cruising at fifty-nine thousand feet. Take a look out your windows. You'll see something very few people have seen: the curvature of the earth."

Maggie turned and looked out the window. From ten miles up, you got an almost chilling perspective of earth. A big, blue-green, vulnerable ball, floating in space, surrounded by nothing.

"A jewel," she said. "It looks like a jewel."

Kleber, his camera mounted on his shoulder, looked through the viewfinder. "Beach ball," he said, and cranked in a ten-to-one zoom lens. "Balloon."

"It's beautiful," she said.

"It's frightening," he said. "One little beach ball in the middle of space."

"And love doesn't make it go round," Palmer said. He looked dour.

Kleber looked up at him. "Oh, yes, it does. Not our stupid romances, no, but somebody sure as hell loves that planet, to keep it spinning for billions of years."

Maggie looked out through the window again, and thought about David, who'd said last night that he had the world on a string.

Harrison looked out the window of his private Piper jet. He was getting a beautiful bourbon buzz. Buzz, buzz, buzz. Bang! A Concorde exploded in his head. He watched it come apart; shards of metal and little doll-like figures moved in slow motion through the back of his mind. He closed his eyes, but this only locked him into the nightmare scene. He reached for the bottle and refilled his glass. There was time to stop it, to phone Robelle and call the thing off.

And then what?

Jail?

Total disgrace?

The end of his work?

He drank quickly.

There was a classic irony for you. His work. A plane that would save men's lives, built on men's corpses. And women's.

He grunted. And what, he thought wryly, was bothering him now, after all this time? What did a few more corpses mean, when you added them onto the total tally? Maggie was right. He hadn't pulled the triggers; he'd just made the guns, the grenades, the launchers, the cannons, and finally, his brilliant Dragonfly. And the death count from all that well-designed metal was in the thousands. So what the hell were a few hundred more? So what if one of them was Maggie Whelan? And so what if Maggie was having his child? He'd have talked her into an abortion anyway, or tried to.

David Harrison: killer of men, women, children, and embryos.

"I'll drink to that."

He refilled his glass and raised it in a toast. "To Maggie," he said. "Sweet Maggie. Who loved not wisely but too well."

Too bad. It was all too bad. An accident. An unlucky accident of history, that Harrison Aircraft was going broke in the year the government was bailing out Grumman, and the public was screaming and Congress was balking at forking out another two hundred million to underwrite the building of the F-14. Now, they thought it was the greatest plane going. The finest fighter in the U.S. Navy, with long-range radar and long-range missiles that could knock out supersonic enemy planes.

But in 1970, the test model crashed. Two more crashes and a dead pilot, and Congress started calling the program a lemon.

And Grumman, with its money tied up in a

lemon, had lost its access to commercial credit. It had asked for a bail-out. And then another. And still it kept raising the price of the plane. The original bid, of eleven and a half million dollars per plane, went up by another six million, and Congress made a law: no more bail-outs.

Iran and Arabia bailed out the project by ordering hundreds of F-14's. But they sure as hell didn't give a damn about a drone. Nobody did. At least not in 1972. The Pentagon thought it was a "hot idea," an "interesting concept," but that's all it was: a concept, an idea in Harrison's mind, which he didn't have the money to build or to test. The banks wouldn't back him, the government couldn't, and that left a man named Andre Robelle.

"A Mr. Robelle on the radio, sir."

The voice seemed to come from the back of his mind—an hallucination.

"Sir? A Mr. Robelle." It was the pilot, his amplified voice booming through the cabin.

Harrison picked up the set beside him. "Put him through, Carter."

"Yes, sir."

There was a short burst of static, then Robelle's clear voice. "David?"

"Andre? Hold it a second. I'm putting this call on the scrambler."

"Bon."

Harrison punched the scrambler buttons. "All right, go ahead."

"I've gone ahead. Our friend Clément should be airborne now."

"Fine. But what about the French Air Force?"

"He's flying under radar. When he makes his attack, he'll have more than four minutes before they respond. He can blast the Concorde in seven seconds and be home for supper before they take off."

"Good. And I'll be in Paris for supper."

"I'll chill the champagne."

"Bonne chance."

Robelle laughed. "No luck needed. It is—as you say in English—in the bag."

8.

Celeste sipped coffee in the galley; this was her first moment of privacy since the flight had begun. Waking this morning with Paul beside her, the first thing she'd felt was an easy warmth, a forgotten feeling of tenderness, the luxury of loving. It had been a long time since she'd felt that way: two years of nothing, of nobody. On only two mornings in all that time had she awakened to find a man in her bed, and neither time had the sex been anything at all but sex—a pointless piece of physical exercise. It wasn't what she wanted. For everyone else, it seemed to be sufficient; other women boasted of "getting lucky," "getting laid," discussed men's anatomies and talked of techniques, as though love were technical, a dance step learned by studying a diagram. The partner was irrelevant, as long as he was limber. But for her, it was different. There was no such thing as sex in the abstract. Sex was Paul—his particular body, his specific smile. It was what he said, and the way he held her, and the sense she felt of *belonging* in his arms. And it was, in 1979, a curse to be a one-man woman like that, when the one man hardly ever came along, and then, if he did, almost always disappeared.

Three rings on the call-button called her to attention; the three-ring code meant a call from the flight deck.

Patroni, on the intercom, told her to make an announcement to the passengers.

She moved from the galley and into the cabin. "Ladies and gentlemen—your attention. We're starting our gradual descent for landing at De Gaulle Airport in Paris. The captain has turned on the seat belt sign, and requests that you stay seated with your seat belts fastened. *Messeiurs et mesdames. On commence la descente . . .*"

Maggie fastened her seat belt and looked at her watch. Another fifty-five minutes to Paris. She reset her watch five hours later, and then looked at the papers again. Some of them—proving Harrison Industries' ownership of Armuco—she understood clearly. It was done through a series of holding companies and dummy corporations. The "president" of one of them was William Halpern; the "owner" of another was "Mariah Wilson," Mariah Harrison's maiden name. The dummy corporations had dummy names (Metals International, Allied Services Company, Inc.), but Metals owned Allied and Allied owned Armuco, and David Harrison owned the whole thing. The connection would have been difficult to prove if one didn't have the documents together in a package.

And then there were papers on Armuco Munitions. Inventory statements revealing discrepancies—fifteen thousand assault rifles missing, simply unaccounted for. And then there was more: lists of figures she didn't understand, papers signed by an Andre Robelle of Service Générale, at a Paris address on the Rue Vaugirard. And finally, blueprints—of God knew what, except that the blueprints bore a label: SCAM. She folded them and put them away in her briefcase.

Palmer came back from the men's room and took his seat beside her.

"A SCAM," she said, as he buckled his belt. "Bob, what's a SCAM? What kind of weapon?"

"Weapon?" he frowned, then shrugged. "New to me." He lit a cigarette. "Sure you don't mean a SAM?"

"No. But what's a SAM?"

"S-A-M. Surface-to-air missile. Usually, it's the Russian-made ones you call SAMs. Technically, they've just got names like SA—, and then a number. The SA-2's a high-altitude missile, with a range of something like twenty-five miles. SA-3, low-altitude, fifteen miles. And the SA-7—that's the one that was used in Iran yesterday—that one's only got a three-mile range."

"And American missiles?"

"What about them?"

She shrugged. "I don't know. What are they called?"

"Hawks, Jerichos. Listen, we've got a lot of missiles." He laughed. "But as far as I know, none of them are con jobs."

Maggie frowned. "I don't follow you."

"Scam," Palmer said. "A scam means a con job, a rip-off."

"Oh. Of course." She nodded slowly; her frown deepened. It still made no sense. SCAM had to be an acronym for something. But for what?

Palmer looked at her querulously. "How come you're asking?"

"Just curious."

"Oh."

"I'm a curious girl."

He grinned. " 'Curiouser and curiouser.' Careful. It killed the cat."

She turned to him. "Hmm?"

"When we get to Moscow, you better not ask them to show you their missiles."

She laughed. "It never entered my mind. I'll ask to see their Gumm's, not their guns."

"Gums?" he asked, and pointed at his teeth.

"Gumm's. The Moscow department store."

"Oh."

"It's across from the Kremlin. You want to come shopping?"

"No." He laughed. "It never entered my mind."

Metrand looked up as the radio said, "Concorde one-one-seven from De Gaulle tower. Continue on a heading of zero-nine-five."

"Roger, De Gaulle." He clicked off the radio, and turned to Patroni. "Home free," he said.

"You're glad to be home."

"Paris?" Metrand said. "I think I'd say this if I came from New York or Rome or Vienna or any-place on earth. Paris is the most out-and-out beautiful city in the world."

Patroni said, "I guess so."

Metrand raised his eyebrows. "You only guess so? You've *been* there, of course?"

"Many times. Yeah. It's just that—well, I don't speak French, and it's always been kind of lonely, you know?"

"Ah! We'll fix that. I'll show you around. I'll find you a beautiful girl who speaks English."

"Hey, would you?"

"One-one-seven," the radio called. "We've been advised of unknown traffic, last reported westbound

146

on a heading of—" The radio died, as though some-one had suddenly pulled out the plug.

Scowling, O'Neill hit the button. "De Gaulle? Do you read me? Hello? De Gaulle!" He turned to Metrand. "We've lost communication."

"Keep trying."

"I am." He kept trying. "No good. We're being jammed."

"What?"

"We're being jammed—somebody's jamming us, that's what it feels like. Come in, De Gaulle. This is Concorde one-one-seven." O'Neill looked up again. "Nothing. Dead."

"Does that sound familiar? A UFO?" Patroni, frowning, looked at Metrand.

"Can't be another drone," Metrand said. "And who'd want to jam us?" Metrand squinted out through the window. Nothing. No traffic. Something unknown was traveling westbound, on who-knew-what-heading, and was who-could-tell-how-many miles to the west.

"Terrorists." Patroni was biting his lip. "The news guy out there thought the first attack was a terror attack."

"Well, it wasn't."

"I know. But this one could be."

"What one? We haven't been—Joe? Are you letting LeBec's little visionary nightmare get you? Because—" Metrand stopped cold. "My God! Two o'clock! Look!"

A Phantom jet—the F-4E.

"He's coming right at us!"

The missile-armed fighter ripped through the sky.

"Full power!" Patroni captained the ship, taking her into a rocketing climb.

The fighter banked and then swooped in ascent.

"Speed!" Patroni yelled. He pushed the thrust

levers forward. They raced, the Machmeter climbing again to Mach two. "He can beat us—outrun us at two point four—and his ceiling is seventy-one thousand feet. He can divebomb us. Jesus!"

"You said you flew one. What does he carry?"

"Sidewinder missiles. Heat-seeking. Four of them. Six-mile range at Mach two-four."

The distance between them was narrowing.

They were over the ocean, and LeBec's bloody nightmare was coming true.

And Metrand's nightmare: the nightmare of war. He thought about Celeste.

"We're in range," Patroni said.

"Sidewinder coming. Five o'clock."

"Christ!" Patroni maneuvered a hard left bank as the nine-foot missile screamed from the wing of the enemy plane. "Violent maneuvers—all we can do. Their seeking angle is thirty degrees. Narrow. There's a chance we can cause—"

A missile raced at the Concorde, aimed at the engines. Patroni pulled into a roll and a bank, narrowly avoiding the missile; it whistled out past them, exploded in air.

"A fly-by." Patroni finished his sentence, and let out a breath. "And the bastard's got three more where that one came from."

"Three more tricks like the one you just pulled, and the plane'll break up. We're not a flying a fighter."

"We'll have to try and send him a false target."

"They're heat-seeking missiles?"

"Right," Patroni said. "O'Neill. The Very gun."

Metrand took the interphone and spoke to Celeste. "We have to depressurize and open a window to shoot off a flare gun." As he spoke, he reached for the oxygen mask that hung from the ceiling over his shoulder. Larger than the masks that would drop from compartments in the passenger section, the pilot's mask looked like a catcher's mask. It contained a microphone. Passenger's masks were released automatically when the cabin pressure dropped; as an added precaution, Patroni flipped a switch.

A bell went off. In the passenger cabin, the masks dropped down.

"What now?" Maggie said, and the plane did another heart-stopping swoop. She forced the oxygen mask to her face.

On the flight deck, O'Neill opened a visor. Wind blasted in and the gun shot out a bright orange flare, as missile number two, heading for the engine, veered downward, hit the flare, and exploded.

"The Air Force," Metrand said. "Three o'clock."

"Nice."

A pair of Mirages, still distant, approached.

But two more missiles had just been fired.

The flare gun jammed as O'Neill tried to shoot.

There was only one thing left to do. "I'm killing our heat source," Patroni said. "Power off."

"Be sure everyone's strapped in tight," Metrand told Celeste.

The engines were killed. Patroni took the plane on a steep-angled dive, almost vertically toward the ocean. The altimeter unwound like a clock, faster and faster—fifty thousand feet . . . forty-eight . . . forty-six . . . forty-four. They were losing eight thousand feet a minute. And gaining nothing.

The missiles pursued.

In the cabin: chaos, terror, screams. The passengers were slammed straight back in their seats; the cabin shook with the force of the dive.

Tatyana, holding her oxygen mask, was suddenly catapulted out of her seat; her belt, too loosely buckled, had come open. She rolled helplessly down

149

the aisle. Palmer grabbed her, clutching her arm, straining to hold her against the relentless force of gravity. The plane rushed downward. He pulled the oxygen mask from his face, and held it to hers.

Cabinet doors in the galley swung open, dishes and glassware tumbled and broke. The door of another cabinet opened. Dr. Stone, the surgeon, looked up and saw it: the thermal container, holding the heart. The container shifted, threatened to fall. For the moment, it held.

Twenty-two thousand feet . . . twenty-one . . . seventeen . . .

Patroni felt the rudder stiffen in his hands.

Metrand took over. "We've got to pull up. She's shaking like a bitch. She wants to belly over." He strained to hold the wheel as the missiles raced past the cooling engines, hitting the ocean, exploding.

O'Neill leaned back and closed his eyes.

"Power on. Engine one." Metrand pressed the starter. The engine whined, sputtered.

The pursuing Phantom fired its cannons.

Patroni laughed grimly. "She's out of missiles. She's on gunpowder now."

"We've been hit," O'Neill yelled. "Our hydraulic system!"

The engine wouldn't catch. They were still in a dive. Metrand kept pushing, praying. The engine hummed, then finally caught. Then the next one started, and the next. The Concorde started to pull from its dive, and leveled out.

The Phantom, in high-speed pursuit, seemed to be struggling, trying to climb. Too low, too fast, too late, it ran out of time, power, and sky.

Smashing into the ocean, it disintegrated.

Patroni took off his oxygen mask. For a long moment he looked at Metrand. "Would you say," he asked slowly, "all things considered, that this was our lucky or our unlucky day?"

Celeste moved around the debris-strewn cabin. She issued orders to the other stewardesses to help the passengers any way they could. Some had passed out from the sudden dive, and a few out of simple, stark terror. The doctor was attending Tatyana Rogov. Celeste checked the thermal container with the heart inside. A miracle, she thought. The straps that were holding it in place had held. Starting to move up the aisle again, she passed by the seat of Eli Sande. His wife, beside him, was sitting with her curly head propped on his shoulder; her eyes were closed. Celeste leaned over. "Does your wife need the doctor?"

Sande looked up, shaking his head slowly. "She's asleep."

"Through all *this?*"

He grinned. "That's my girl."

Celeste looked around at the other passengers. Starting to fight through their shock and their fear, they were now asking questions. Metrand's announcement—"We have no information on who attacked us. We're waiting for landing instructions from De Gaulle"—had accomplished little. The questions continued.

"Mr. Sande," Celeste said, "perhaps if you explained?"

"Explained what?"

"Well . . . anything. They saw those missiles. And they certainly know we went into a dive. Maybe if you told them why—or something. Anything that sounds official."

"Yes," Sande said. "I believe you're right." He followed her to the intercom phone at the front of the cabin. For a moment he stood there, tall, straight, white-haired, relaxed.

151

"Folks," he said slowly, "I run this airline, and I want to tell you this is not a typical flight."

There was a ripple of relieved laughter.

"But if anything," he went on, "it ought to increase your confidence in flying. You've just seen—" he smiled—"and felt—some of the finest piloting in aviation history." He looked around. "We don't know who attacked us. Terrorists, obviously. But what cause they intended to forward by blowing us up has yet to be revealed. They attacked us with heat-seeking missiles. Such missiles are drawn to anything hot. And our engines are hot. We take in air that at high altitudes is minus sixty degrees centigrade, and when it leaves the compressors, it's plus five hundred and fifty degrees. And if you don't understand centigrade, that's over a thousand degrees Fahrenheit. But that's not all that's hot. When you're traveling at supersonic speeds, the skin of the plane gets hotter than the boiling point of water. The more you slow down, the more you cool down. So that's what we were doing—slowin' down, goin' down, and cooling off fast. And your pilots were pretty cool-headed guys. We dodged those missiles and we're safe. And for that, I'd like to thank God. And our pilots." He paused. "And the Concorde. I don't think we could have made it in any other plane." He cleared his throat. "And we ought to be landing—" He looked at Celeste. "When?"

"The captain said fifteen minutes." She added, "We'll be landing at Le Bourget instead of De Gaulle."

For a fraction of a second, Sande indulged himself in a puzzled frown. Then he smiled again. "Well, now." He spoke in his usual, booming voice. "Now that's a treat. We'll be landing at the airport where Lindbergh landed. And it's even closer to the heart of Paris. Cheaper cab fare." Sande made another reassuring smile. Turning to the hand mike, he whispered to Celeste, "Anything the matter?"

She beckoned him into the flight deck.

III

1.

There were reporters all over the field, from *Le Monde, Figaro,* all the dailies, from *Match* and the other weekly magazines; and from the three television channels. There were policemen, military guards, and men in plain clothes from the DST—the French FBI. It all added up to confusion, shoving, noise, heat, and the constant whirring and flashing of cameras.

Maggie pushed her way through the crowd, clutching her briefcase. A French reporter, his mike in his hand, rushed up to her.

"Madame—s'il vous plaît. Vous avez atterré—"

"Yes, we've landed," Maggie said briskly, "and it feels wonderful, if that's your question. How else would it feel?"

The reporter nodded. He was tall and bespectacled. His microphone, labeled *Antenne 2,* showed he was the Channel Two newsman from Paris. "Do you know what the attack was about?" he said in English.

"No. Do you?"

He shrugged. "Four terrorist groups have taken credit. They claim it's a protest against the Olympics. Or rather, three of them do. The fourth one says it was part of yesterday's strike in Iran. Anti-American. What do you think?"

"I think," Maggie said, "that the world has gone mad. Now if you'll excuse me—" She pushed through the crowd to the baggage claim counter, as the Channel Two newsman turned with his mike.

"Ah! Voilà le capitaine américain." He pushed his microphone at Joe Patroni. "We heard you had some trouble landing, Captain. We heard your hydraulic system was hit."

"One of them was. But as you probably know, a Concorde has three hydraulic systems. No single hit could knock them all out."

"Then why did you land at Le Bourget instead of De Gaulle?"

"For security reasons. If someone was after this particular plane—and it sure as hell looks like it, doesn't it?—well, they might have been waiting to hit us at De Gaulle."

"Yes. That makes sense," said the newsman.

"Does it?" Patroni answered. *"None* of this makes any sense to me." He moved from the microphone, shaking his head as another reporter, this one from *TéléFrance 1,* was busy cornering Eli Sande.

"Yes," Sande snapped. "Of course we're going to Moscow tomorrow. I'll be damned if anyone'll stop this flight!" He hurried angrily away down the corridor, holding tight to his young wife's hand.

Another reporter rushed up. "Madame Sande, what are your reactions to this terror attack?"

"I slept through it."

"What?"

But Sande had whisked his wife out of range.

"*Comment?*" said another reporter to the first.

"*Elle a dormi,*" the first one answered incredulously.

"*Impossible!*"

"*Oui? Pour les américaines, tout est possible.*" He shrugged.

Arnie Kleber came in through the gate, his camera running, recording the scene: cops, reporters, passengers, chaos. His camera focused on the thermal container that, with luck and skill and speed, would be saving the life of an American child. He focused on Palmer and Dr. Stone.

"It seems to be safe," Dr. Stone was saying. "And I think we have just enough time to make it from here to the hospital at Neuilly."

"Good luck."

"Thanks," Stone replied. "We'll still need that." He was holding Mrs. Gaminsky's hand. Together, they rushed to the waiting ambulance.

Palmer looked around for Tatyana, and spotted her walking with Nelli. She was limping slightly from her tumble down the aisle of the plane. He got to her side just as Nelli was saying, "It's only twisted, but you'll have to stay off it for twenty-four hours."

"My ankle," Tatyana showed it to Palmer. It was slightly swollen.

"I see," Palmer said.

Nelli said sternly, "She'll have to stay in bed."

"I see," Palmer said, and grinned at Tatyana, who flushed a little, then grinned back.

". . . and boeuf bourguignon," O'Neill was saying, "and *frites,* very salty, and a gallon of wine and three cups of coffee."

Celeste laughed. "Seems like you're going off your diet?"

O'Neill walked behind her down the steps of the plane. "Listen," he said, "it occurred to me up there that there's no guarantee that I'll live to be a hundred. I could've gotten blown away right in that cockpit and it wouldn't have been because I'd eaten a steak. So what the hell? I mean, Jesus, *rabbits* only eat vegetables, and *they* don't live to be a hundred either."

Metrand walked beside them on the tarmac now. Moving up to Celeste, he whispered, "Still mad?"

She looked at him. He was infuriatingly handsome. She shrugged. "I thought it was unnecessary to boast to Joe."

O'Neill moved away.

"Yes," Metrand agreed. "If I'd told him about us, it would have been a boast. And not a sexual boast. Not 'look who slept with me,' but 'look who's my woman.' "

"I'm not your woman."

"I know," he said. "And you ought to know I didn't say anything to Joe. He was joking. He told me what a great time the two of you had in Georgetown. I told him I'd gone directly to sleep. And that's what he meant when he told you I'd had an 'exciting night.' He was joking. Now, you know him. He's a kind, shy man, Celeste. Do you think if I *had* told him, he'd try to insult you? Make a leering remark?"

"Oh," she said. "I guess I was—"

"Looking for an excuse to get mad at me?"

She studied him slowly. "Maybe you're right."

O'Neill was waiting in front of the gate. "We're wanted for debriefing," he said. "In there."

They joined Patroni in a quiet room. *Entrée Interdite,* said a sign on the door.

160

An hour later, they had given all the facts they knew to the French authorities. They were all seated together around a vinyl-topped table, drinking coffee.

"That's all?" said Inspector Lucas to Metrand.

Metrand replied dryly, "I think that's enough. Any ideas who did it?"

"Too many ideas." Inspector Lucas lifted his shoulders. "Too many confessions, too many possibilities. We're investigating all of them. But that takes time."

"I think the plane should be kept under guard," Metrand said, "while the crew's going over it making repairs, and right up to takeoff."

"And when will that be?" the inspector asked.

Patroni shrugged. "Whenever all the repairs have been made."

Lucas nodded. "According to the maintenance manager here, when she's ready to fly, they'll ferry her out to a shed at De Gaulle. You'll take off from there."

"Bon." Nodding slowly, Metrand stood up. "If that's all, Inspector . . ."

"Yes. But if you think of anything else—any other detail—you'll call me?"

"Of course."

Lucas turned to Celeste. *"Et vous, Mademoiselle.* You can call me any time at all."

In the corridor, heading for the exit to the bus stop, Metrand took Celeste by the arm. "Listen," he said, "I promised Joe we'd give him a tour of Paris tonight."

"We?" Celeste said. She looked at Metrand, then turned to Patroni. "We'd be happy to, Joe."

Patroni smiled. "That would sure be nice."

Metrand added quickly, "And I'll get you a date. I know someone perfect. I absolutely guarantee you'll fall in love. We'll pick you up at nine in front of your hotel."

Automatic doors opened in front of them. The evening was chilly and gray. Paris. *Paree,* Patroni thought. Everyone loved it, but for him it had always been just another town. The streets were more beautiful, but just as lonely, filled with unknown faces and other people's laughter, and the days always ended in the same dark bars, with the bottles lined up in the same neat order as in Cincinnati or Phoenix or Rome. Only somehow, in Paris it hurt a little more. He took in a deep breath of cold air, letting it out as a tired sigh. And then it occurred to him that he didn't have a long, empty day ahead of him. It was almost seven o'clock at night.

They boarded the bus marked Porte Maillot.

"No, that's a bus for the airport personnel," Palmer said to Nelli. "And your bus is probably waiting at De Gaulle. Why don't we drop you off?"

"Sure," Kleber said. "I just rented a Fiat."

"No," Nelli answered. "We travel with the team."

"Well, we can't take the whole team with us in a Fiat." Kleber laughed heartily—one of his most phony laughs. "But I was only thinking of Tanya's ankle. The sooner she gets it soaking in a tub . . ." Kleber let the words trail off.

Tatyana looked at Palmer. Palmer cleared his throat. Nelli looked at Palmer darkly, suspiciously. Palmer almost said, *And we can't make love in a Fiat, either, not with three other people around. So what are you worried about, you old biddy?* But he held his tongue.

Nelli said, "Yes . . . you may have a point. All right. We are staying with the rest of the team at Cité Universitaire. On the campus. Do you know where that is?"

Kleber nodded. "To hell and gone. Near the Parc Montsouris. At the back end of Paris." He looked at Palmer, narrowing his eyes. Outside the big double doors of the terminal, raindrops were starting to pommel the ground. In rush-hour traffic, and adding the rain, the drive could easily take an hour and a half.

Palmer got the message. As a former quarterback, used to calling the plays, he tried to think quickly of what play to call. It wouldn't be fair to kill Kleber's night. And they both had to be at a television studio to do a quick turn at eleven o'clock. Their words—and Kleber's film—would be beamed by satellite over the ocean, and make the "On The Spot" newscast at six. He was thinking of trying to rent his own car when the blue-and-white bus pulled up to the curb.

"That's us," Nelli said, as the rest of the team members started to rise.

Tatyana looked at Palmer, and said with a trace of sadness, "I'll see you tomorrow."

"I'll carry your bag."

Gregori stepped in front of her. "And I carry you," he said, and lifted her up as though she were a doll. Palmer followed, holding the bag.

"Arnie?" Maggie called.

Kleber turned.

"I don't want to be rude, but do you mind if I just take a taxi to town? I sort of want to be by myself for a while."

"Sure." Kleber studied her. "You okay?"

She shook her head. "No," she said matter-of-factly.

He nodded. "I know what you mean. Shall we call you for dinner?"

"No, I think not. I'll just order room service. You can pick me up and drive me to the studio, though."

"Right. We'll leave at ten thirty. Okay?"

She nodded. *"A tout à l'heure."*

"Huh?"

"See you later." She smiled. "I'm practicing my French."

2.

There was a queue for the taxis. There seemed to be half a dozen people ahead of her, and soon there were half a dozen people behind. It was raining softly, more like a heavy mist than a rain, but the dampness mixed gloomily with the chill in the air. Maggie closed the top button of her coat and pulled up the collar.

The line moved quickly. There was one man ahead of her. No cabs in sight.

Finally, a taxi turned up the ramp and pulled to the curb.

The man in front of her turned and smiled. *"C'est le vôtre,"* he said, and opened the door.

"Non," she protested. *"Vous êtes—"* She'd forgotten how to say "You were first." *"Vous étiez—"*

"Oui," the man nodded. *"Mais vous êtes belle. S'il vous plaît, Mademoiselle."* And Maggie smiled, getting into the cab. In Washington, a man wouldn't let you have a taxi just because he happened to

think you were pretty. She'd forgotten Frenchmen as well as French.

"Hotel Ritz," she said to the driver.

He started the motor. *"Américaine, huh?"*

"Oui." She hoped he didn't speak any English so she wouldn't have to start making conversation.

"Vous parlez français?"

"Non," she said.

"Ah! Dommage! Je ne parle pas anglais." He lit a Gauloise and that was that. It was a radio cab. He reported his destination and the time. Then there was silence.

Maggie leaned back, taking a breath, closing her eyes to the heavy traffic of the Autoroute du Nord, and the garish high-rises ringing the road. She'd forgotten how aggressively ugly they were, and there were more of them now, higher and uglier. It was hard to understand why people did ugly things on purpose.

And why would *David* do something ugly? It didn't make sense. He had money, talent, brains, luck. Why would he have to do something ugly? And yet there were the papers, locked in her briefcase, and Carl Parker, locked in the morgue. But David had said he wanted to explain. How *could* he explain? Could there be an acceptable explanation? Or maybe . . . maybe things weren't what they seemed. Maybe the papers were circumstantial evidence, proving nothing. Maybe— She laughed dryly to herself. "There are a thousand maybes," McKeever had once said, "in every case that I've ever worked on. And the fastest way I know of to drive myself nuts is to name more than seven maybes at once."

Which left her five more maybes to go.

Maybe David was being blackmailed or threatened, or was working undercover, helping the government to trap someone else. Maybe Parker had forged the papers, or used them as a cover to steal the blueprints, and maybe the blueprints—

No. That was already seven. *Stop,* she told herself. *You'll know the truth in a couple of hours.* She looked at her watch. If he'd left Washington at ten this morning—adding the five-hour difference in time—he ought to be in Paris by ten tonight. She could use the intervening hours to drive herself crazy or to try, somehow, to let herself relax. And relaxing, at least, could leave her with a little reserve of energy to take the next blow—if that was what was coming.

Lighting a cigarette, she looked through the window. The city ahead of them, night-lit now, was the same breathtaking place she remembered. They'd left the highway at the Porte Maillot. Ahead was the lighted Arc de Triomphe, and L'Etoile, the huge, circular island crowned by the Arc, with ten major avenues radiating out from it, just like the beams of light from a star. L'Etoile: the Star. They circled around it, then continued down the Champs-Elysées. The traffic was heavy, the sidewalks jammed; there were lines in front of the movie houses, one of which was showing *L'Arnaque—The Sting.* There were crowds at the Drugstore, crowds at McDonald's, crowds spilling out of the shopping arcades, browsing at the windows of Yves St. Laurent and Charles Jourdan. The cab turned left past the Tuileries gardens in back of the Louvre, and finally into the Place Vendôme, the large, wide, circular "square" rimmed by the curved, pillared palace of the Ministry of Justice, and across from it, the columned façade of the Ritz.

Inside the Ritz, the lobby was long and narrow. There were tables, chairs, palm trees in pots, vases on pedestals, flowered carpeting.

The clerk said, "Madame?" with a tentative smile,

a twitch of the lips; a *polite* little twitch, it proclaimed that, after all, the owner of those lips had smiled at countesses, exiled kings, and Elizabeth Burton. "And your name, Madame?"

Maggie showed her passport and claimed her reservation.

"You'll be staying with us for only one night?"

"Yes. That's right."

He pulled a key from a board behind him. "Room 327. It faces the court." He examined her passport; she filled out the forms. A tall man waited at the side of the desk, checking his watch.

"Monsieur?" said the clerk.

"Finish with the lady," the man said in French.

The clerk called a porter, then turned back to Maggie. "Yes, Miss Whelan. Anything else?"

"Yes. I'm expecting a friend later on. Mr. David Harrison. I'll be in my room till at least ten-thirty. If he comes after that, will you tell him to meet me at TéléFrance One, Studio A. And one other thing. I'd like to take a nap. Will you see I'm awakened at a quarter of ten?"

The clerk made a note, then turned to the man who was waiting at the desk. "Monsieur?" he said, as the porter was leading Maggie away.

The man asked him where the telephones were.

my son's in college. How about some coffee,
Celeste?"

"Of course."

3.

It was ten after three, Washington time, when the
telephone rang on McKeever's desk.

The call was from Paris: Claude Benet, from the
lobby of the Ritz.

He reported that Maggie had been driven to the
hotel by an Agency cab, and was staying in room
327. He assured McKeever that the room would be
watched.

"She also left a message at the desk," Benet said.
He repeated the message.

"Hold it." McKeever squinted at the phone.
"David Harrison's going to Paris?"

"Unless he plans to visit by ESP."

McKeever was checking the clock. "I'll tell you
who else I want you to watch. Andre Robelle."

"You want to explain?"

"You don't have enough dimes."

"What's Harrison got to do with Robelle?"

"That's what *I* want to know. And someone had better watch the airport for Harrison's plane."

"Bien. Is that all?" Benet asked sarcastically.

"Tell me what you've got on that 'terrorist attack.' "

Benet was silent for a moment. "You sound like you don't think it *was* a terrorist attack."

"Maybe it wasn't. Maybe lightning strikes twice."

"I don't follow."

"That plane was gone after twice. The first attack came as it was leaving Dulles. And you know by what?"

"No. By what?"

"By David Harrison's drone."

Benet whistled.

McKeever continued, "The Bureau got a call from a kid named McGuire, a technician at Harrison. Just before the drone started heading for the Concorde, its chief designer was tweaking the computer. Just *after* they'd listened to the Concorde's headings. McGuire was suspicious."

"What does that mean?"

"Probably nothing. Or at any rate, nothing we can *do* anything with. But our 'Man of the Year' starts to look like a very interesting man indeed. His head salesman was killed last night at Miss Whelan's house, by a man who resembled Anthony Cooper. This morning, Harrison's drone attacks her plane. It's attacked again off the coast of France. And now David Harrison's leaving his home, and his Man of the Year award presentation, and flying to Paris. Interesting, yes?"

"But what does it mean?"

"I don't know," McKeever said. "I've been chewing on so many half-baked theories, I'm getting indigestion. But I do know this: I want Maggie Whelan watched. Every second."

"That may be difficult. What if she wants to go to bed with—"

"She probably will," McKeever interrupted. "But he won't try to hurt her. Not if there are witnesses around."

Benet thought it over. "I follow you," he said.

"You're a genius, Benet. I'd never have thought of what you just thought of."

"Va-t-en foutre."

"I love you too." McKeever laughed. "And I'll see you at eight-fifteen in the morning."

"What's that supposed to mean?"

"Air France flight number 502."

"You're coming to Paris?"

"You're not a detective for nothing, Benet."

"How did you work it?"

"I didn't work it. I'm coming to Paris at my own expense. I have some days off. I'm a jet-setter, Claude. Two days in Paris. I do it all the time."

"A bientôt, mon vieux."

"Yeah. See you soon."

4.

Sighing, Palmer hung up the phone. He turned to Kleber, who was lying on the bed, on the white cotton spread with his dirty sneakers on, while he did a few sit-ups on the creaky mattress. His cigarette dangled from the side of his mouth, dripping ashes on his curly brown beard.

"She's staying at the Maison Grecque," Palmer said. "The city university doesn't have dorms; it has little houses, little residence houses where students of different nationalities stay."

"So? She's staying at the Greek House. So?" Kleber fell back, exhausted, on the pillows.

"So she's sharing a room with the fair and beautiful Comrade Nelli."

"Who's locked her up and thrown away the key."

"Something like that. The doctor said her ankle will be perfectly fine if she just stays in bed for twenty-four hours. Christ! We've got only a week together and we're missing Paris."

"What the hell," Kleber said. "Paris isn't much of a town for lovers."

"Funny." Palmer was pacing the floor. He paced to the window. From their room in the front of the Hotel Colbert, he could see Notre Dame.

"All right," Kleber said. "So what do you say we shower, get dressed, and pick up some pastry at the *Deux Magots*."

"I'm not hungry," Palmer said.

"Right. Only dense. I wasn't exactly speaking of food."

"I know."

"Oh."

Palmer sprawled on the bed across the room. "There's got to be a way to get Nelli to leave. She won't leave the room, not unless we can think of—"

"We can't," Kleber said.

Palmer mused, staring at the ceiling, "What if Nelli got an invitation to see the town? The 'educational' parts of town. You ever see *Ninotchka*? Remember when Garbo—"

"Nelli isn't Garbo."

"You can say that again." Palmer turned his head and looked out the window at Notre Dame. "Maybe we could take her to church to pray?"

"For what?"

"Tanya's ankle?"

Kleber just looked at him.

"Right," Palmer said. "So maybe if a dashing American photographer—"

"If that's *me*, I'm dashing for the nearest exit."

"Right," Palmer said. He looked at his watch. Ten after eight. He'd be through at the studio by eleven-thirty. He could be at the Greek House at midnight. "What could get Nelli out of that room?"

"A major earthquake," Kleber suggested. "Orders from Brezhnev. A rabid tiger that escaped from the zoo and—"

"That's it!" Palmer said.

"A rabid tiger?"

"A bear," Palmer said, and reached for the phone.

Joe Patroni reached for the soap, lathered himself, and then let the steamy water from the shower splash directly on top of his head. He noticed he was humming—and then noticed *what* he was humming: "Got a Date With an Angel." It suddenly depressed him. First of all, the song was a 'forties song, which made him feel old, and secondly, the song was an optimistic song, which made him feel stupid. And what made him think his date would be with an angel?

Paul Metrand.

Paul had said, "She's a beautiful redhead. She's intelligent, charming, about thirty-eight, and she speaks perfect English."

"Which is more than *I* do," Patroni had said.

"Allons donc! Nonsense!" Metrand had retorted. "What you really need is more confidence, Joe. You're a beautiful guy. *Un brave mec."*

Stepping from the shower, Patroni studied himself in the mirror. "Beautiful," was not exactly the word. Twenty pounds overweight, with a faceful of lines. Unlined, it hadn't been a winner either. He looked, he thought, like an old, beefy, red-faced cop. He was big and awkward, and worst of all, for a man of his age, he was shy with women. He flushed, was tongue-tied, tripped on his own feet. And since Marie had died, there'd been no one in his life. Mostly because he hadn't tried. And he hadn't tried, mostly because he was certain he'd fail. The only place he felt sure was a flight deck. He could keep his cool under flak and fire with four engines out and the rest of the crew and the radio dead. He'd done that once, in the South Pacific. But put him a room with a beautiful woman . . .

Relax, he told himself, as he started to shave. *Paul and Celeste will be right there beside you. And maybe,* he thought, to cheer himself up, *maybe this "date" won't be beautiful at all. . . .*

It was a small bedroom on the top floor, with a fireplace, a rocker, and dormered windows. Nelli was sitting, reading, on the rocker. Tatyana lay propped on one of the beds, her swollen ankle resting on pillows. Outside the window of the Maison Grecque was a small, dark, tranquil park, which wasn't Tatyana's idea of Paris. She'd pictured lights, gaiety, crowds.

Nelli could sit there quite contentedly, reading a book, but Tatyana, leafing through *Elle* magazine, only felt a deepening disappointment as she looked at the pages of Paris fashions—the pictures of laughing women and men, running in the parks, walking on the bridges, caught in a kiss beneath a yellow umbrella.

She looked up slowly at the knock on the door.

Nelli jumped up. "I'll get it," she said, and opened the door.

Gregori stood there blushing, holding a big bunch of flowers.

"For Tanya? How lovely." Nelli took the flowers. "She's feeling much better. Won't you come in?"

Gregori, still flushing, shifted his weight and entered the bedroom with careful feet, as though he thought the floor underneath him might break.

"How nice of you, Gregori," Tatyana said with a warm smile. "Please. Sit down."

Gregori looked around for a place to sit down. He shot a mistrustful glance at a chair and decided to just keep pacing the room. He looked out the window. He cleared his throat. Tatyana and Nelli exchanged a shrug.

"I was going out to have dinner," he said. "I wonder if you want me to bring something back." He now looked at Nelli. "You have not eaten, have you?" His tone seemed to make it an urgent question.

"No," Nelli said.

"Aha!" He smiled. "Then you come with me. We bring something back for Tanya."

"Oh, no. I shouldn't leave her."

"Oh, please, Nelli. Go," Tatyana burst out. "I mean—it's fine. I'm not in any pain. And you ought to see Paris."

Nelli shrugged, indifferent to Paris.

"As a favor to me then," Gregori pleaded. "My little one, she is already asleep and Sonia Bellinski is watching her, *da*? And for me—" he sighed, a gigantic sigh— "it has been a long time since I have an evening with a beautiful girl."

Nelli looked at him as though he were crazy. Nelli was far from beautiful. She was slim and limber, but that was all. Her features were heavy, and her iron gray hair was cropped close to her head.

"You remind me so much," Gregori said gently, "of my long-dead wife, my dear Natalia."

Tatyana looked up.

Something marvelous happened: Nelli blushed. "Well . . ." She seemed almost ready to relent.

"Oh, do," Tatyana said. "You would make me so happy. You could look at Paris and tell me about it."

"I would not be gone long," Nelli said, *"if* I went."

Tatyana took a quick look at her watch. It was 9:15—too late for Robert to get here and back in time for his broadcast. And Nelli would never stay out past midnight, which might be the soonest he could get here at all. Still, a little privacy now was worth something. At least she could talk to Robert on the phone. It was really awful that she missed him so much after only two hours. "I'm not at all hungry," she added quickly.

"And Sonia has plenty food," Gregori said. "You get hungry, she share with you. Come," he said to Nelli. "We never have chance to see Paris again. And me? I kick myself hardest of all for things I have not done, not what I *have* done."

For a moment Nelli looked at him slowly, and the big, bearlike weightlifter smiled.

Nelli nodded. "All right. But just for a while."

"Da!" He grinned, clapping his hands. "I meet you on street in half of an hour."

When he had left, Nelli ran a hand through her hair and looked at Tatyana. "Why does he think I would need so much time? All I have to do is put on my coat."

"Oh," Tatyana said. "But why don't you put on my pretty pink dress? And some lipstick, Nelli. Oh, Nelli, why not?"

"No," Nelli said. "That is foolish business."

"Isn't it time to be foolish? Just once?"

"I have told you, I have been foolish. Just once, with my swimmer in Rome. And once was enough."

"Was it really?"

"Yes," Nelli said, and tightened her lips. She reached for her coat. "I'll return in an hour."

5.

Robelle was waiting on the airfield. As the Piper taxied slowly toward the hangar, Harrison could see him standing in the rain. Robelle was unchanged, still slightly dramatic in his black rain cape, his hat cocked at a rakish angle on his head, and a fat cigar glowing in the dark. They met at the edge of the tarmac.

"*Ça va?*" Robelle asked.

Harrison laughed. "It goes pretty badly, by the look of things. Doesn't it?"

Robelle shrugged. "We've been through a lot worse." They crossed the field to where a chauffeured Daimler was parked behind a yellow Mercedes sedan.

Harrison smiled. "You hired me a car?"

"But of course."

"And the driver? Is he one of your men?"

Robelle shook his head. "No. He comes from the car-hire service. The fewer connections between us, the better. I'm afraid the *flics*—the, how you say, 'cops'—are aware of the men who work for me."

"Oh?" Harrison frowned. "Since when?"

Robelle laughed. "Ever since they hit on our friend Dauphin and broke up our . . . warehouse in Reims. They have nothing on me. But I still behave cautiously. *C'est emmerdant,* but what can one do?"

"It's more than boring," Harrison said. "It could be dangerous."

"It hasn't been yet," Robelle countered hotly. "The only danger so far has come from you. Leaving papers in your office was damn stupid."

"Agreed. But it's done." They'd walked to the door of the yellow sedan.

"Come into my car and we talk," Robelle said.

Harrison nodded and got into the car. The interior smelled of expensive leather and expensive cigars. Robelle pulled a silver flask from a compartment. "Cognac?"

"No. I just got sober; I don't want to undo it. There's a problem to discuss."

"Yes." Robelle drank directly from the flask. Lit only by the field lights, his face looked puffy. "And how do you intend to . . . dispose of our problem?"

"Has Cooper come back yet?"

Robelle looked up. "No. Your friend Halpern had him stay for a while. He'll be back this evening. Why? You want him to do another job?"

"Maybe. But it has to look like an accident. A random accident. And I'm still not sure it's a good idea."

"Right. It's a bad idea," Robelle said. "To kill her in Paris starts making a link between Paris and Washington, Parker and Whelan, and sooner or later, between you and me."

"Yes. *D'accord,*" Harrison agreed. "So what do you suggest?"

"I suggest the lady is a good pear."

"What?"

"Une bonne poire."

"Oh. You mean a sucker."

"Yes. This lady is a sucker. I suggest you give her *du boniment.* 'Hand her a line,' is that how you say it?"

"Yes, I suppose I could do that. Sure." Harrison smiled. "The lady is very often naive."

"Fine. You just keep her happy. *Fais du boniment. Fais de l'amour.* And let the 'terrorists' take care of the rest. Oh, yes." He smiled into Harrison's frown. "It seems the same group who struck in Iran attempted to shoot down the Concorde today. I heard it on the news. So it wouldn't really be so hard to imagine they might try it again, now would it?" He drank again from the flask.

"Nor hard to imagine they'd fail again, either," Harrison added. "It seems they've failed twice before."

"Yes. But they tried to attack in the air."

"There'll be guards at the airport," Harrison said. "We can't fake a 'terror attack' on the ground."

"No. I don't mean that sort of attack."

"Then what do you mean?"

"Sabotage."

"How?"

"I own a certain man. One Carl Froehlich, a member of a terrorist group from Berlin. He's been waiting undercover in Paris for a year. Would you like to know what Froehlich does for a living? He works on an aircraft maintenance crew. One of his co-workers happened to suffer an unfortunate accident this evening and Froehlich just happened to take his place. Repairing the Concorde."

Harrison laughed. "You're a genius," he said.

Robelle nodded. "In my own way—yes."

"How will it be done?"

"Explosive decompression. Sometime during

flight, a door inexplicably flies from its hinge, blows open in midair, and the difference, of course, between the normal air pressure inside the cabin and the near vacuum we have outside—*vlan!* The Concorde, she breaks apart."

"Not necessarily."

"Fft!" Robelle sniffed. "The sun will not necessarily rise, but the chances are excellent, wouldn't you say? And then—just in case—Mr. Froehlich can 'fix' a few other things too."

Harrison nodded. "Sounds pretty good."

"Yes. We should not meet again, *mon ami*. We have to be careful. I'll keep in touch through the regular channels."

Nodding, Harrison opened the door. "All right," he said. "I'll work on the lady, you work on the plane."

"Agreed," Robelle said. "Au revoir, *mon ami*."

Harrison walked to the waiting limousine.

Metrand pulled his Fiat into a side street near the Place de la Bastille—a narrow street, only one block long, with a string of ancient apartment houses. Rain fell softly. The street was clogged with traffic. Somebody pounded hard on a horn. A fat man sitting in the Volvo in front of them stuck his head out and shouted, "Ta gueule!"

"What number is her house?" Celeste turned to Metrand.

"Seven."

Lucky," Patroni muttered. "What's her name again?"

"Gabrielle Barleducque."

"We'll go up to her apartment, or what? Or she'll be downstairs, or what?"

Metrand looked over his shoulder at Patroni. "I'll run in and buzz her, and she'll come right down.

There's no place to park." He smiled. "Will you relax?"

"I *am* relaxed," Patroni grumbled.

Celeste turned the car radio on. *"Comment trouvez-vous le temps chaque jour,"* a voice inquired, *"de prendre soin de votre ménage?"*

Metrand and Celeste both started to laugh.

"What's so funny?" Patroni asked.

Metrand turned the dial to music. "It said, 'How can you find the time every day to take care of your house?' "

"That's funny?"

Celeste turned around. "Oh yes. I discovered Paul trying to clean up his studio for me. He'd swept all the dustballs under the bed. So then he reached under it to fish for his shoe, and it came out looking like a furry gray cat." Celeste was laughing.

Metrand shook his head. "She stood across the room, and—no kidding—she said, 'Paul? You have a cat?' "

Patroni laughed. "Well, at least it shows he doesn't have a woman. A woman doesn't let a man live like that."

"Yes. Or he has one," Celeste said quickly, "and he lives at *her* house."

"I don't," Metrand said. "And here's number seven." He pointed out the window. "I'll be right back."

"That!" Gregori was pointing at the wine list. He looked at the waiter. "Big of it," he added, indicating "big" by the spread of his hands.

The waiter approved. "A fine champagne." He bowed his retreat.

"Champagne?" Nelli said.

"Why not? We're in Paris. We get a little happy. Why not? We get drunk. Why not? Hah?" Gregori laughed. *"Mozhno.* It's allowed, yes?"

Nelli shrugged. "I don't get drunk."

"Never?"

"Never. You will be drunk much sooner than I."

"What?" He laughed again. "You are tiny woman. Me, I am bear."

"I never get drunk," Nelli repeated, and looked at her watch.

Tatyana picked up the ringing phone. "Robert?" How are you? *Where* are you?"

"In a phone booth. Listen, I'll try to be there by midnight."

"No good. Nelli will be back."

"She's with Gregori."

"How did you know?"

"A hunch. The same one that tells me she'll be gone all night."

"Oh, Robert, that's impossible."

"Nothing's impossible." He paused for a moment. "I'll call you at eleven—just to make sure."

Hand in hand, they raced through the rain. Gabrielle took Patroni's hand, and her hand was soft and warm. And she *was* beautiful. Exquisite, amazing. Ahead of them, Metrand and Celeste made a dash through the door of a restaurant.

Gabrielle laughed. "They're winning the race."

"Come on!" Metrand hollered from the doorway. "Come on." He held the door open. Patroni, still holding Gabrielle's hand, made it through the door.

"Paris always rains on me," Patroni complained.

Metrand pushed his fingers through Patroni's wet hair. "He looks cute when he's wet, huh?" He turned to Gabrielle. "He reminds me a little of a happy fish."

"Yeah? What kind of a fish?" Patroni said.

Gabrielle looked up at him. "Well, not a shrimp."

Patroni laughed.

"You two take a table," Metrand said quickly. "I know the *patron*. I'll have him cook us a special meal." He turned to Celeste. "Come with me and charm the pants off DuVal. He'll put extra beef in the boeuf bourguignon."

She laughed. The two of them walked to a table at the back of the room, where a round little man in a waiter's apron rose to embrace them.

"Old friends," Patroni said, taking in the scene. He was suddenly aware that he sounded wistful. He blushed, which only made it worse.

"Come on over here," Gabrielle said. "There's a table by the fire."

"Nice," Patroni said. Sitting, he looked around slowly at the room. It had a beamed ceiling, a fireplace, red and white tablecloths, candlelight, flowers, and a pastry cart.

"You are soaking wet," Gabrielle said. Picking up a napkin, she dried her own face. He watched her, and felt himself blushing again.

"A happy fish." She tilted her head. "You are adorable when you're embarrassed."

He lit a cigarette. "Then I must be adorable a hundred times a day."

"You are easily embarrassed?"

He shrugged.

"You are shy," she said. "The best men are shy." She looked at him steadily and nodded. "And the best men are always married. Yes." She nodded again. "You look married."

"Yeah? What does a married man look like?"

"Mmm. His smile says 'no,' and his eyes say, 'when?' "

Patroni smiled and said to her, "When?"

She arched her eyebrows and took a cigarette.

He leaned forward to light it. "I *was* married, Gabrielle. For twenty-five years. My wife is dead. Two years ago."

184

"I'm sorry."

"Yeah. So am I."

"You miss her."

"Very much."

She studied him slowly, blowing out smoke. "You have any children?"

"A son. He's starting college this fall."

"Ah." She smiled. "My boy, he is starting university too. The Sorbonne."

"College? You don't look old enough."

"Hah. *Grâce au maquillage.*"

Patroni laughed. "Did you just call me a liar?"

"No. I just said, 'Thanks to makeup.' "

"Well, you don't owe it *too* much thanks. You're . . . beautiful," he said.

"Clean living," she said, and looked down, studying her hand. Looking up quickly, she said, "And your son—what does he study?"

"Medicine. Pre-med."

"Yes? A coincidence. So does my Philippe." She smiled. "We have a lot in common, Captain." She put her hand softly over his.

6.

"Talk about 'On The Spot News,'" Palmer said, staring at the red eye of the camera. "That's where Maggie and I were today. And the spot was sixty thousand feet in the air. That's where we were when the terrorists attacked FWA's flight one-seventeen. Reports as to who those terrorists were are still unconfirmed, but French counter-terror authorities believe it's the work of the group that struck in Iran. We have no further word on that at this time." He swiveled in his chair. "Maggie? I leave it to you to describe exactly what it was like up there."

A camera beamed its eye on Maggie. "We were attacked by an F-4 Phantom jet, armed with four Sidewinder missiles. It was war up there—passengers screaming, missiles exploding around us in the air. And in order to dodge them, the plane had to dive." Beyond the camera, she could see the control room, and David, watching her. "It was expert piloting, the work of a team of . . ."

* * *

Harrison listened. Her description was concise, vivid, and terrifying. He felt his throat tighten. He grabbed a container of coffee from the console. It was old, cold coffee. He drank it in a gulp. Over a film taken in the Concorde during the attack, a tape recording ran, echoing screams and prayers.

And then Maggie was moving away from the desk. The studio lights were dimming.

He rose, left the control room, and met her in the hall. He moved to embrace her.

She stood rigid and unyielding in his arms. She was still confused and uncertain, afraid of trusting her desire to trust him.

"Thank God you're all right," he whispered. "I couldn't—I couldn't imagine losing you."

His blue eyes scanned her. She found them as hard to read as the sky; they were clear and cloudless. But terrible things could come from out of the blue. She moved away from him, lowered her eyes. "You said you had something you wanted to explain. I'm listening," she said.

"With an open mind?"

"Oh, it's open, all right." She laughed ruefully. "In fact, I think I've got a hole in my head. I read those papers. I believe them, David. And still, I haven't done a damn thing about them, except wait for you to tell me I've got it all wrong, that black isn't black and white isn't white." She looked at him pleadingly. "Tell me, David."

"I love you," he said.

"That's irrelevant."

"Is it?"

She stared at him. "Yes."

He winced. "I've got a car. We'll talk over dinner."

"I've eaten."

"Okay, then we'll go for a walk."

She nodded.

"Pont au Double," he said to the chauffeur, and they rode in silence till they got to the bridge, then walked across it slowly. A *bateau mouche* passed underneath; strains of music floated from its deck.

"I won't lie to you," he said. "Not anymore. I was trying to save face, I guess. Or my good name. I was also trying to save my work." He looked at her, frowning. "That work is important, Maggie. The Dragonfly project is good. It's a very important weapon—important for the government. It's not an aggressive weapon, it's defensive. It can save a lot of lives, spare a lot of pilots. I keep thinking about my brother. He was flying a fighter in—"

"David, don't do this."

He stopped, and leaned against the railing of the bridge. "Do what?" he said.

"Change the subject."

"The subject is why I did what I did. That's part of the answer."

"Then you *did* do it."

He lit a cigarette, and looked down at the Seine. He was silent for a while. Finally he said, "My father used to say, 'Success is in the right hand of God.' Well, *I* was in the right hand of God. Only I was too young, too successful for my own good. Right out of Harvard, I invented a wing structure. 'Revolutionary,' they called it." He laughed dryly. "A few years later, my father was dead, my brother was dead, and I found myself running a billion-dollar business. And a few years later, I found myself running it into the ground."

He started walking again. She walked beside him silently. From across the bridge, they approached Notre Dame.

"Unfortunately," he said, "my father never mentioned the left hand of God. That's the one that puts the squeeze on you. I couldn't get money, Maggie.

So I started rationalizing. What the hell, you know? The world's up to its neck in weapons as it is. The government's selling them to anyone who'll buy, or almost anyone. And I thought, in the general destructive scheme of things, what difference would a few more assault rifles make? Jesus. In the black markets of the world, you can buy yourself a couple of cases of grenades as easily as you'd buy yourself a case of champagne. All you have to have is the money, Maggie. And I had to have the money." He turned to look at her. "Can you understand that?"

She shook her head slowly. "Maybe because I've never had it."

"It wasn't the money for the money's sake. It was for the project's sake."

"Are you saying the ends justify the means?"

"No, Maggie. It wasn't justified, and I know that. I've know that for a long time. But once I got caught up in that—in that world, I was caught. Trapped. You can't get into that and then get out of it by saying, 'Sorry, I changed my mind.' Or you're likely to find yourself facing . . . what Carl Parker faced."

They were standing in the park in back of the cathedral. Its stained glass windows gleamed, vivid in the night.

"Are you saying Parker was part of it?"

He nodded. "And he wanted to get out. And he did . . . didn't he?"

She stared at him. "Are you saying the same people who killed Parker would try—"

"To kill me?" he interrupted. "Who knows? Probably. Or my children. That's been threatened before."

"Then what will you do?"

"The only thing I can do: I'll spring the news myself. But you've got to give me time, Maggie. Time to get protection for my family, to get them someplace safe. Then I can call a press conference and make a statement myself. Once I've admitted this publicly, once they know I've already talked to the feds, there isn't any purpose left in killing me, or hurting my family. You see?"

She nodded. "I . . . I think so."

"Then will you let me handle it my way?"

"I don't want you to get hurt."

He laughed. "Honey, I'm going to get hurt no matter what. The point is, I suppose, it's like cutting out a cancer. I've got to do it. Then maybe my life can heal itself, you know? And maybe I can start all over again. But whatever life I have, Maggie, you're . . . you're a very important part of it. You . . . and our child. I don't think I could do this if you weren't here, if you didn't love me . . ."

"Oh, David." She could feel the tears on her face.

He held her and kissed her, in front of the windows of Notre Dame.

7.

"I don't believe it." Tatyana giggled, kissed Palmer again, and then giggled again. They rolled over on the bed. "How did you know Nelli would stay out? Robert?" She pulled away from him, frowning. "Did you have something to do with this?"

He grinned. "Well, I did make a call to Gregori . . ."

"And what did you say?"

Palmer was laughing. "I asked him if he could lift a weight off my back. C'mere," he said.

But Tatyana's frown deepened. "Oh, dear."

"What's the matter?"

"I was thinking—poor Nelli. I mean, you know, I think she was . . . well, she was flattered, pleased, you know, that he asked her to go out. Not that she showed it but, oh . . ." She rolled away from him. "Men are so cruel sometimes to women."

Palmer ran a finger down the bridge of her nose. "You know what Gregori's first answer was? He said. 'No. She wouldn't go out with me. She little bird. What she want with big ugly bear?' "

"That's what he said?"

"Yeah. He likes her. And you know, sometimes women are cruel to men."

She looked at him quickly out of the corner of her eye.

He nodded. "Like a guy can be nuts about a girl who won't marry him and won't leave him alone."

"You want me to leave you alone, Robert?"

"No. I want you to marry me, Tanya, and I can't—I can't get through to you, can I?"

She was silent for a moment. Closing her eyes, she put her arms around him and, sighing, buried her face in his chest. "Would it help you," she asked finally, "to know that I will never love anyone else?"

"No," he said. "That'll just hurt me more. I don't understand this. I don't understand."

"Yes you do, Robert. The same way you feel about your country, I feel about mine. It isn't perfect, but it is my home, my people, my language, my culture. It is terrible to be without a country."

"Yeah? Well, I think it's worse to be without love. That's the only country worth living in, Tanya. Look, forget it. Never mind. I'm sorry I started it."

She stroked his hair. "You are very romantic for a football player."

He rolled over on top of her.

"I love you," she said.

He nodded, and then all he said was, "Hush."

Patroni opened the door of the bar—the famous Harry's New York Bar—and stared for a moment at a roomful of noise. The place was a saloon—an ordinary, grimy, noisy saloon, seven-to-a-block on Lexington Avenue. But here, it was special.

He looked at Gabrielle, and then at the lineup of hot-eyed studs at the long wooden bar. A couple of them yelled out snappy remarks. Patroni didn't have to understand French to know what they were saying. A beautiful woman entering a bar on Lexington Avenue would get the same act: "Bébé! Oo-la-la!"

He took her by the hand, protectively, proudly, and pushed through the crowd. They walked down a flight of stairs at the right, to a smaller, equally noisy room, with a few dozen tables and an upright piano, where a Frenchman played Gershwin, not very well. Patroni ordered Scotch; Gabrielle, a Pernod.

One bar ago, at the Closerie des Lilas, Celeste and Metrand had called it a night. Patroni checked his watch. It was two A.M.

"Are you tired?" Gabrielle asked.

"No," he said quickly. "It's still only nine o'clock by my head."

She nodded, smiling. Her hand reached for his. "And what time is it," she said, "in your heart?"

After a moment, he said, "It's been bedtime for almost an hour."

She smiled wider. "I don't really want that drink very much."

"Neither do I."

"Shall we go?"

"Gabrielle?"

"Yes?"

"I want you to know something."

"Yes."

"This has been the nicest—the finest—the best damn evening I've had in years."

"It will get even better, dear Joe."

"I know. I just want you to know how I feel."

"Thank you," she said, and he noticed that her eyes were starting to mist. She rose abruptly and said, "Let's go home."

*　　*　　*

McKeever unfastened his seat belt, stretched, and lit a cigarette. The stewardess handed him a little toy bottle of Cutty and a glass, and a little silver packet of nuts. "A dollar," she said.

He'd just written out a check to the airline that would easily have covered the deposit on a boat he'd been wanting to buy and that would now stay a dream for another few years. What bugged him was having to pay for the drink, and what *really* bugged him was the fact that, at the grizzly age of thirty-seven, making out a check for six hundred dollars still represented financial suicide.

He handed over a hundred-franc note.

The stewardess frowned at it. "Sorry," she said. "I don't have the change. I'll catch up with you later."

"That's what they all say." McKeever grinned, and pocketed the note. How To Get A Free Whiskey On An Airplane: present a big bill. On the other hand, getting your gun onto a plane wasn't nearly that easy. Three interviews, forty-five forms, and then he'd had to totally dismantle his revolver and hand it to the captain, who'd keep it during the flight. Sure, there were ways to beat the regulations, but they weren't worth the trouble. Especially not since the trip was unofficial.

Sipping his whiskey, he wondered exactly what the hell he was doing, and why, and for the seventeenth time in a row he came up with the same unacceptable answer: he was following a strong, half-illogical hunch.

And the hunch was followed by a second hunch: on Monday morning he'd feel like an idiot. And not only that, but like a *broke* idiot.

He sipped his whiskey, and leaned back in his seat.

* * *

David Harrison leaned back in the seat of the chauffeured Daimler. Even in the dark, with his eyes closed, he was conscious of Maggie studying his face. His arm was around her. He pulled her closer. He felt her relaxing; her head rested on his chest, and strands of her hair tickled his chin.

"The Ritz," the chauffeur said. Harrison quickly opened his eyes. *"Vous voulez que j'attende?"* the chauffeur continued.

Harrison looked at Maggie now. "Well?" he said. "Shall I tell him to wait?" He looked deeply into her eyes. "Or to go?"

She was silent for a moment. She sighed. "To go."

"You can go," he said. "Pick me up in the morning at eight o'clock sharp. We'll be going directly to the airport."

The chauffeur, nodding, held open the door.

In the lobby, a tall, well-dressed woman walked up to Maggie. "Why, Maggie Whelan! My goodness!" she gushed. She turned to Harrison. "And I know who *you* are," she beamed. "David Harrison, the American airplane genius. How delicious."

Maggie looked puzzled.

"Well, don't you remember me? Caroline Walters," the woman went on. "We met at Dior. You were covering a show. Well, anyway, you *are* looking divine. Won't you come with us? We're off to Montmartre." She gestured broadly at a group of five: two other well-dressed, middle-aged women and three exceedingly fit young men.

Maggie declined sweetly.

Caroline smiled. "Well, I just can't wait to write that I saw you. You know I do the 'People' column for *Soir*." She added, *"Bonne nuit,"* as opposed to *bon soir,* which showed that she was aware they were going to bed.

"I'm sorry," Maggie said, as they walked up the

stairs. "They'll be gossiping all over Paris tomorrow."

Harrison winced. His hopes for anonymity were totally gone.

The best laid plans, he thought wryly, and looked at Maggie as she opened her door.

Metrand padded barefoot through Celeste's familiar, orderly apartment. He opened her refrigerator and filled up a large wineglass with milk.

Walking back to the bedroom, he stopped in the hall and examined the framed pictures on the wall: Celeste's parents at their farmhouse up north; her sister and brother-in-law on the beach; her three-year-old nephew, who would now be five, looking frightened to death on a carousel horse; Celeste and a rather good-looking man, posing on the Spanish Steps in Rome. The picture made him frown. Who was that man? And why the hell was he smiling like that? Still frowning, drinking his wineglass of milk, Metrand continued to study the wall; there were two pictures of him and Celeste. One had been taken at the casino in Monte Carlo on their last trip together. He'd never seen it. He remembered she'd had a camera with her and had stopped a stranger, asking if he would take their picture. The second picture he remembered well. It had been taken during the weekend they'd spent at the Château de Pray. Metrand had taken it; she'd set the camera and run like hell to appear in the picture. It showed the two of them, laughing on the banks of the Loire.

"Hey," she was calling from the bedroom now. "Did you get lost or something?"

"Mmm," he said, and entered the room, still sipping his milk.

She looked at him and laughed.

"What's funny?" he asked.

"A stark naked man drinking milk from a wineglass always amuses me."

"Oh," he said flatly.

She was sitting up in bed. She'd pulled the covers up over her chest.

"Do you see such things often?" he said.

She didn't answer.

"Who is the man in that picture?" he said, suddenly conscious that he looked ridiculous, pacing, jealous, naked—and holding a glass of milk. He put down the glass.

"What picture?" she said.

"On the Spanish Steps."

"A man," she said, tilting her head, "who asked me once, 'Who is the man in that picture?' 'What picture?' I said, and he said, 'The one on the banks of the Loire.' "

"And what did you tell him?"

" 'An old friend,' I said."

"And who is he?"

"An old friend," she said.

"How old?"

"I'd say about thirty-seven."

"Amusing." He wheeled. "I meant, how long since you've been with this man? Or are you still with him?"

She was silent again. "Would you care if I were?"

"You're damn right I would."

She was laughing.

He was furious. "Goddamnit! I love you!"

She stopped laughing and stared at him.

He said it again quietly. "I love you, Celeste."

Still she said nothing, just stared at him, then tilted her head. "As long as I've known you, you've never said that. Why now, Paul? After all this time."

He moved over to the bed, and sat on the edge of it. "Today, when we were playing with death up there, I suddenly started to think about life. About really living it, not just walking through it, you know? Or running away from it."

"And what has that got to do with me?"

"Everything," he said. "I—" he sighed— "I want to start living, Celeste. And that means I want to start living with you. I'd like us to try again. What do you say?"

She took a deep breath. "Ask me again tomorrow," she said. "If you still feel the same way."

"I'll still feel the same way."

"Sleep on it," she said, "and we'll talk tomorrow."

He looked at the clock: 3:25. "Then I guess I'd better get to sleep. Fast." He got under the covers beside her, holding her. *"Je t'aime,"* he said. *"Je t'aime, je t'aime."*

"Nous verrons," she said, curling up. "We'll see."

Maggie awoke in an empty bed, and for just a second, before her mind was completely awake, the pain and horror of the last few days seemed vague, like part of a shadowy dream.

She came fully awake as she heard the sound of the shower in the bathroom, and then, turning, she saw David's watch on the table, his clothes on the chair, and she remembered clawing at his back. "You're hurting me," he'd said, and she'd answered, "I hope so. I want to hurt you."

She closed her eyes, feeling the full brunt of despair. She'd said, "I love you. *Why* do I love you?" She hadn't known the answer; she still didn't. But now, as she listened to him splashing in the shower, she started, painfully, to question the question. *Did* she love him? Or was loving him a habit—something she'd been doing for so many years, it was automatic, reflexive, and totally unreflecting? She had loved him, but why? Because their life together had been smooth, undemanding. She'd loved him because he was matter-of-fact and clever and charming. And together, they were so damn terrific in bed.

But not last night. Last night all she'd felt in his arms was . . . alone. And it suddenly occurred to her that the man she'd been loving was not the actual David Harrison; she'd only been in love with whomever she'd *thought* David Harrison was.

And what was he now? Liar. Sell-out. Opportunist. The ugly words shoved through her mind. *Weak. Immoral. Treacherous.*

Killer.

His weapons had been killing thousands of people.

She forced herself to think it again: *killer.*

He walked through the door with a towel wrapped around his waist. "My flight's in an hour. I've got to get going."

She nodded.

He frowned. "You feeling okay?"

"Fine." She watched him starting to dress.

"And what time's *your* flight?" he asked.

"I don't know. We were scheduled to leave at three-forty-five. But they said they'd call if the plane won't be ready. At any rate, we'll be in Moscow by tonight."

"What did you do with the papers, Maggie?"

"Why? What difference does it make?" she said.

"You've got some things there that the Russians might be all too interested to know. And they'll be pretty thorough when they check through your bags—not to mention your room."

"You never explained those blueprints, David. Is that what you're worried about? The blueprints of the SCAM? What's a SCAM, David?"

"A government project. And that's what you'd better not take into Russia."

She furrowed her brow. "Why did Parker have it?"

"How the hell do I know?" he snapped at her. "Sorry." He softened. "It's going to be a rough day, Maggie. I'm going back to face a lot of nasty music. I don't know everything Parker was up to. But the blueprints have nothing to do with the rest, I swear. Let me have them back, will you, Maggie?"

"I can't."

"You don't believe me?"

"I—I think I *do* believe you, David. But I left the papers in the studio vault."

"Where we were last night? That studio?"

"Yes. I left them with a tape. If you haven't done what you've promised to do by the time I get to Moscow, I'll—"

"I will. I told you."

"If you haven't, I'll call and they'll broadcast the tape."

"Not tonight, Maggie. Don't do it tonight."

She sat up in bed. "Oh, David, don't tell me you're copping out, *please*. I—"

"Honey," he laughed. "Arithmetic was never your longest suit. Remember, it's seven hours later in Moscow than it is in Washington. When it's midnight over there—"

"Oh," she sighed, and then smiled at herself. "You're right. Arithmetic isn't my forte."

"I need time to fly home, to get my family to someplace safe, and to get in touch with someone in the government. Only after that can I make a public statement." He strapped on his watch. "By the way, you said you had a friend at the Agency."

"Did I?"

"Yes. On the phone, back home. You said I could trust him."

"Yes."

"What branch does he work for?"

"Counter-terror, I think."

"Well . . . that sounds perfect." He nodded. "What's his name?"

She hesitated for only a second. "Johnson," she said. "Alfred Johnson."

8.

Benet was waiting for McKever at De Gaulle. McKeever got his gun back—in several pieces—and Benet filled him in.

"Busy night," Benet said. "Your girl's okay."

"Not *my* girl," McKeever said quickly. "Go on."

"Harrison's gone. His plane took off half an hour ago."

McKeever grunted. "You tailed him in Paris?"

Benet had a pudgy ironic face. He squinted at McKeever. "Harrison's chauffeur was one of our men. We also managed to follow Robelle. And bug him."

McKeever looked up. "Bug, as in 'bother'?"

"Bug, as in 'give him a *micro-manchette*.' You know what this is? We put a microphone into his cufflink. When he holds up a telephone to talk . . ."

McKeever laughed. *"Formidable!"*

They walked across the lot to Benet's battered car.

"Go on," McKeever said when he'd settled in the seat.

For answer, Benet hit the button of a Sony cassette recorder. A tape started playing.

"The papers," said a voice. It was American, male. "In a studio vault at TéléFrance One."

"C'est fait," said a Frenchman—Robelle. "We'll take care of it. Anything else?"

"No. How's your end?"

"Everything's done. Part two will be accomplished at four-twenty-five."

"Good."

A pause.

"It was very costly," Robelle said slowly.

"What's money?"

"Quite so. He collected last night. He'll be flying to Rome."

McKeever looked up at Benet, who shrugged.

"And you," the American said. "I think you should warn our friend in Strasbourg."

Again McKeever looked at Benet, who grinned.

"It's done," Robelle's voice continued on the tape. "However, he wasn't very worried. *Bon voyage.*"

"Thanks. Keep me posted."

The tape ended.

"That was from a phone booth," Benet added. "An hour ago."

"Not bad," McKeever said.

"Not *bad?*" Benet's round, apple-cheeked face creased in a frown. "We have hit the jackpot and you say 'not bad'?"

McKeever nodded. "*Good* would be if we knew who was going to Rome, exactly what he did to earn a fat sum of money, and exactly who and what to look for in Strasbourg."

"On the other hand—"

"Yeah," McKeever interrupted. "If that was Harrison—"

"It was."

"I figured. So we've got a link between him and Robelle. We can pick up some papers from a Téléfrance vault, probably put there by Maggie Whelan, and a neon arrow is pointing to Strasbourg. But to *what* in Strasbourg?"

"The depot, *mon pote,* where they're storing the arms."

McKeever laughed. "We aren't that lucky. Come on, let's go."

"Where to?"

"Where to? To the papers in that vault."

The note said:

> Got hungry and the cupboard was bare.
> Bought you some milk, butter, croissants.
> Left them in the kitchen.
> See you later.
>
> Paul

Reading it, Celeste felt a terrible temptation to cry.

There it was. A love letter from Paul Metrand, to rival the love notes of Barrett and Browning.

Instead of crying, she laughed. That was that. In the cold light of morning, he'd changed his mind, couldn't wait to get away from the scene of the crime, didn't want to meet her eyes, didn't want to explain. So he explained without explaining. Absence, after all, speaks louder than words.

She put the note back on the bedside table. There was only one consolation in this: it wasn't unexpected: she'd had the foresight, the self-control, or the pessimism, cynicism—maybe just realism—to say to him cooly last night, "Think it over." It wasn't much of a consolation, but if it didn't spare her pain, at least it saved her pride. When she met him again—it would be on the flight deck, not before that—she could simply be arch, or a little one-up. (Of *course* I didn't believe you. I *told* you I wouldn't take you seriously, Paul.")

But standing in the kitchen, looking at the potful of coffee he'd left, and the croissants on the table, she closed her eyes for a short, sad minute, thinking how nice it would have been to have breakfast together, and make love again. As the coffee heated, she looked out the window.

The day was sunny. The streets would be filled with couples, lovers. A day for a woman alone to stay home.

Through the window of the taxi, Maggie looked at the sunny Saturday morning in Paris: the market-place streets, with their stalls of fruit, vegetables, fish, and flowers; the lines in front of the bakeries; the crowds of people, walking in the sun with long loaves of bread tucked under their arms and bright canvas shopping bags loaded with cheese, wine, a poulet for dinner, a treat for dessert. And then, once again, she thought of McKeever: the weekend shopping they'd done together; the dinners she'd cooked on his terrible stove; the silly picnics they'd had by the Seine. . . .

The cab turned into the Rue Vaugirard, passing the ugly Montparnasse Tower—fifty-six stories of glassy modern, sticking out like a sore glass thumb—and then they were heading west toward the Seine. Finally the driver turned his head and said, *"Nous voici.* Here we are."

And there they were, in front of the television studio.

"Thanks." She paid him and entered the modern

building, showing a pass to the uniformed guard at the door.

"Whom do you want to see?" he asked her.

"Monsieur Ravignol, the head of security."

The guard shook his head. "He is not here now. There is no one in his office."

"Is he expected?"

"Sooner or later."

She hesitated, then pulled an envelope out of her bag. "Will you give this to him—to no one but him—and tell him to put this with the rest of my things?"

"Oui, Madame."

"It's very important."

"Of course." He yawned and put it in his pocket, a man who knew the things women thought were important: running out of butter, scorching a shirt.

"Very important," Maggie repeated.

This time he glared at her.

"Thank you," she said, and walked back out to the sunny, empty, Saturday morning.

Tatyana woke up at the sound of the door opening very slowly. It creaked.

"Good morning, Nelli," Tatyana said loudly, and Nelli almost jumped to the ceiling, then actually blushed!

"I just went out for an early-morning walk," Nelli said brusquely.

"And you made your bed neatly before you went out."

"Of course."

"Of course, of course." Tatyana giggled. She sat up in bed, cupping her knees.

Again, Nelli flushed.

"Oh, tell me about it," Tatyana said. "Come on, Nelli. We're all girls together, aren't we?"

"Hah! I am hardly a girl."

206

"With the right man, every woman is a girl. Tell me about it. Start with Paris. Where did you go? What did you see?"

"Did you know," Nelli said, sitting down on the bed, "that Gregori is really very nice man? Very kind, very gentle. Did you know he had read all the classic writers? A surprising man. He is very surprising." Nelli stood up and paced to the window. She suddenly laughed. "I told him I could drink him under the table."

"You *what?*"

"Oh yes. We start with champagne. We later drink vodka. We drink all night. We talk and drink, drink and talk."

"That's all?"

Nelli smiled. "My generation is different from yours."

"Oh." Tatyana shrugged.

"The difference is, we don't *discuss* the other things."

"Oh." Tatyana looked appraisingly at Nelli. "Well . . . for a person who drank all night—or *most* of the night—you look very sober."

"I am."

"How's Gregori?"

"He's fine." Nelli laughed. "Sleeping like a log. You know, I did something I have never done before. In the drinking contest? I let him win. I pretended to pass out. He carried me home."

Tatyana smiled. "So you won, didn't you?"

Nelli shrugged. "Maybe. We'll see."

There was a note in the envelope:

M. Ravignol—
Please put this tape in the vault with the envelope I left you last night. I may call you tomorrow evening from Moscow to

ask you to play it. Many thanks for your
help.

Maggie Whelan

In Benet's sunny office on the Quai des Orfèvres,
McKeever put the tape cassette on a deck, and
pushed the button.

Maggie's voice said, "Monsieur Ravignol, David
Harrison of Harrison Aircraft has assured me he's
planning to inform the authorities of certain illegal
transactions in weapons. If you're playing this tape,
it's because he hasn't done so. And so I'm asking
you to take the documents you're holding in the
vault and turn them over to—well, I suppose to the
American embassy, and tell them I plan to broadcast the story. That's all. And again, thanks for your
help."

Benet looked up. "That clears her of withholding
evidence, doesn't it?"

"I guess," McKeever said. "She's also got the
First Amendment working for her." He glanced
again at the papers on the desk. "But there's nothing in here that might put Harrison in jail. It proves
he's the owner of Armuco Munitions, which we already knew, and that Armuco has an office in Paris.
Shipments between the two branches aren't illegal.
The branch in Paris sold various weapons to a
French distributor. That's legal too. Some weapons
are missing? He could say they were stolen, or in-
ventoried on another piece of paper. He's in
business with Robelle, but we've never had enough
on Robelle to take action." He tossed down the papers. "And we still don't. Harrison could come out
smelling like a rose."

"He's guilty as hell," Benet said grimly.

"I think so too. And so does he. He's running
around like a headless chicken. But the papers alone
don't prove very much." McKeever picked up the

blueprints and studied them. "SCAM," he read. "What the hell's—?" He stopped, flipped a few pages, and said, "Holy shit!"

"What?" Benet said.

McKeever started laughing. "If this is what I think it is, Claude, we've got him."

"What is it?"

McKeever stood up. "Let's get hold of someone who knows about missiles."

"Where are you going?"

"To have breakfast. If anything breaks, I'll be at Select."

Benet raised his eyebrows. "There are twenty cafes right around the corner. Isn't Select a long way to go?"

McKeever nodded. "Even longer than that. A sentimental journey." He paused and shrugged. "If Robelle's men try to break into that vault, if you locate Cooper, or if anybody shifty tries to take off for Rome—"

"I'll call you."

McKeever nodded. "Right."

Out on the street, he glanced back quickly at the shadowed arches of the Palais de Justice. In front of him, the Seine, and shimmering in the sun, reminded him of other, lazier days.

He took a bus down the Boulevard St. Michel, and then walked along Montparnasse to Select.

Metrand hadn't slept. He'd lain next to her, wrapped in her arms and his own promises, and watched the night tick away on the night table clock.

Maybe he did love her, but at five A.M. it seemed irrelevant. At five A.M. he was alone in the dark with his own nature, or second nature, and his own habit of not loving.

At 5:30, as he turned to look at Celeste, asleep,

with a a smile on her face, he was vaguely aware that the accurate name for his feeling was fear—fear that he didn't love her, mixed with the even worse fear that he did.

Well, he thought, she'd told him to sleep on it; he hadn't slept, and by 6:45, it was clear that he wouldn't.

The store on the corner opened at seven. He'd shopped for them both and then gone home to bed, falling asleep on top of the covers, instantly.

Now the telephone rang. With his eyes still closed, he reached for it, answered it.

"Paul?"

He opened his eyes. "Joe?" He looked at the clock. It was after eleven.

"I didn't think you'd be there," Patroni was saying.

"Then why did you call?"

"On the chance that you would be. Listen, you were right."

"About what?"

"You guaranteed that I'd fall in love."

Metrand sat up suddenly. "Joe? Are you serious?"

"I think so." Patroni paused. "She's wonderful, Paul. I just left her. She was going to church."

"To church?" Alert now, Metrand rubbed his jaw and groped for a cigarette. "Where are you now?"

"I don't know. I took a bus. I'm calling from the street."

"What street? I'll meet you for breakfast—or lunch—or—"

"Wait a second. I'll look." Silence.

Frowning, Metrand smoked his cigarette, dropped some ashes on chest, and cursed softly. Patroni came back on the line. "Boulevard Montparnasse. At the corner of the Rue de Rennes."

"You're right near me. You know where to find

the cafe Rotonde? Walk down Montparnasse, about two blocks. It's a few doors down from the Cafe Select. I'll meet you there at, uh—give me half an hour."

"Anything the matter?" Patroni said.

"No. Is anything the matter with you?"

"No. Everything's perfect."

And that's what's the matter, Metrand thought, sighing. "See you soon."

"Yeah. *A bientôt.*" Patroni laughed.

"The plane's okay." Metrand pulled a chair out and sat at Patroni's table in the sun, under the awning. "I just got a call. It's fixed, under guard, and waiting at De Gaulle. We'll take off on time. Three-forty-five."

Patroni looked at him. "You look like hell."

"You're pretty, too."

"You feel okay?"

"I'm fine. I just haven't had very much sleep. After lunch, I'll go home and nap for a while. *You* look fine."

Patroni smiled. "Yeah. I didn't get much sleep either."

"I figured."

The waiter came. "What do you want?" Metrand said.

"Fried eggs and bacon and a toasted bagel."

"Very funny." Metrand ordered two cheese omelets and bread, *"Et deux grand cafés, tout de suite, s'il vous plaît."*

"I don't know," Patroni said, his big frame teetering back in his chair. "I never believed in love at first sight, but that Gabrielle—she's really, really something special."

Metrand had thought it over, and had decided the best way to do it was quickly, lightly. "She ought to be special," he said. "For twelve hundred francs."

For a moment, Patroni just stared at him. Then he leaned forward slowly. "You mean . . . you mean she's a—"

Metrand nodded. "Yeah."

Patroni stared for another second, then he suddenly laughed out loud. "You goddam sonofabitch," he said.

"I thought it was what you needed."

"It was, it was. The joke's on me."

"I didn't mean it as a— Jesus, Joe, I just thought you'd know."

Patroni was still laughing. He seemed okay. He was taking it in stride. "Twelve hundred francs— that's about what? Three hundred bucks?" Patroni pulled a wad of bills from his pocket.

"It was a 'welcome to Paris' gift, Joe. I don't—"

"Hold it! Gabrielle gave me this money to give you. She said it was a loan and she was paying you back."

Metrand looked up, "You kidding me?"

"No." Patroni smiled. "Which makes it the best damn gift I ever got. Hey!" Patroni pointed. "Isn't that what's-her-name? Maggie Whelan?"

"Where?" Metrand turned.

"You missed her. She just walked into Select."

9.

The story was on the front page, and it was yesterday's news. A Concorde had almost been downed over the Bay of Biscay, by a group of terrorists. Of the four groups confessing to the crime, the authorities were more or less zeroing in on the group that had struck before in Iran. Their attack plane, they claimed, had been based "on the northern border of Spain, in a secret airfield."

Maybe. McKeever put down the paper and finished his coffee.

"Encore de café?" the waiter asked. His name was Jean, and McKeever remembered him. The waiter, an old, leathery man, smiled, adding, "It's been a long time." And turning, holding McKeever's empty cup, he added, *"Voilà!* And here is Madame."

McKeever followed his glance to the doorway.

Maggie stood there, looking around.

For a second, McKeever felt two separate emotions: embarrassment at his own stupidity for choosing, of all the cafes in Paris, the one where he and Maggie used to go; and he was a little stirred, touched, flattered, that of all the possible cafes, she'd chosen it too. And then the two feelings jumbled together into one, and all he was left with was a feeling of stupidity. Because why the hell would she even remember? And what the hell would it mean to her? And on top of all that, she'd spotted him now and was coming his way, when he hadn't wanted her to know he was in town.

Terrific, McKeever. Nice going.

She stood in front of him, her head cocked to the side. "If this is a coincidence—"

"It isn't. Sit down." A new ballgame, McKeever thought, and it called for new rules.

"Did you follow me?" she asked.

"No. How could I follow you? I got here first."

"I meant to Paris," she said, sitting down.

He nodded.

"Why? Because of Carl Parker?"

"Nope."

"Why then?"

"If you're hungry, the Croque Monsieur here is good."

"Luke?" She looked at him with her big blue eyes. Her yellow hair was parted in the middle and caught in a pair of coral barrettes that matched her sweater and the color of her lips. "Don't you think I'm entitled to know?"

"No," he said, and lit a cigarette. "But you're entitled to guess. I'd like to hear what your guesses would be."

She lowered her eyes. "Stop playing with me, Luke. If you don't want to answer, just say 'no comment.'"

"No comment." He smiled. "Now what would you like to eat?"

"Nothing. Just coffee."

He watched her, feeling grimly amused. Since she'd seen him, she'd turned about three shades paler, and didn't seem to know what to do with her hands. Or her eyes, for that matter. They stared at him, dropped, stared at him, dropped. He glanced at the window. The agent who'd been tailing her had noticed McKeever, and had opened a *Tribune* and started to read, his elbow poking through the window of his car.

"Do you think I'm guilty of something?" she blurted.

He looked at her again, his face a parody of puzzlement, his eyebrows arched, and then creasing in a frown. "Would I have a good reason to think so?" And now her discomfort twisted into pain and he wanted to reach for her hand across the table. Instead he repeated flatly, "Would I?"

"No," she said, and did not meet his eyes.

Jean came back and made a fuss—how nice it was to see her again, how beautiful she looked, how pleasant to see, in this quick-changing world, that beauty and love could still remain constant. He beamed at them both, gave her the coffee he'd brought for McKeever, and went off to get more.

"You *are* constant, aren't you?" McKeever said slowly. "Loyal, I mean. Constant and loyal."

"Sounds like a dog."

"No. It sounds like an English tea. Constant & Loyal, by appointment to His Majesty."

She laughed in spite of herself. "I've never known how to read you," she said.

He nodded. "Uh-huh. Ever heard the name Andre Robelle?"

"No."

He nodded; she was telling the truth.

"Marc Dauphin?"

"No."

215

"How about Stanley Sylvano?"

She frowned. "That sounds familiar." She pursed her lips, tilting her head. "Wait a second! Wasn't he the Boston Bomber?"

"Uh-huh."

She stared at him, sunlight bouncing all around her hair. "I don't understand."

"Think about it. Have you ever heard David mention anyone in Strasbourg?"

"No." She frowned. "Stanley Sylvano put a bomb on a plane that was leaving Logan. He wanted to kill his mother."

"Or Reims? David ever mention anyone in Reims?"

"No. He's never mentioned anyone in France." Her eyes flashed. "What the hell are you insinuating, Luke?"

"Nothing," he said.

"You think someone put a bomb on the Concorde?"

He shook his head. "It's been guarded by an army ever since it arrived. And before it takes off, they'll go over it again with dynamite sensors and bomb-sniffing dogs."

"Then what were you implying?"

"Nothing," he said.

She continued to glare at him. Her anger showed that she'd gotten his drift; a desperate man could blow up an airplane as a way of murdering someone on board. But there wasn't anything McKeever could add. Everything else was bluff, hunch. A technician at Harrison had a suspicion that couldn't be proved. McKeever, in finding the papers in the vault, suspected what Harrison's motives might be. And Harrison's proven link to Robelle could also be a link to the Phantom jet that had attacked the Concorde on its way into France. Added together, that,

and a dime, wouldn't even buy a cup of coffee anymore.

He squared his shoulders. "I have to explore everything, Maggie. It's my job." He looked at her
levelly. "A lot of people's lives were at stake on that
plane."

"And what's that got to do with David Harrison?
And Strasbourg? And Reims?"

"I don't know," he said honestly. "That's why I'm
asking."

Jean came back with the coffee. McKeever peeled
the paper from a sugar cube and dropped it in the
cup.

"What are you working on, Luke?"

"What are you hiding, Maggie?"

She didn't answer.

"Suppose I told you that the first attack on the
Concorde yesterday was made by David Harrison's
drone."

"I'd say it was a lie."

He nodded slowly. "Constant and Loyal, attor-
neys for the defense. I'm telling you the truth." He
handed her a clipping from yesterday evening's
Washington Star.

She read it, looking pained, stunned, frightened,
then finally relieved.

"It says it was an accident. The Harrison tower
reported it immediately."

McKeever nodded. "So it says," he said.

"That isn't the truth?"

"Oh, sure. It's the truth—as they told it."

"And what's the Gospel according to Saint
Luke?" she asked sarcastically.

"Think about it yourself. You've got a good
mind, I always said so, Maggie. You heard it here
first."

She looked at him harshly. "I don't believe what
you're implying."

He suddenly grinned. "You've got a lot of company. Neither does my boss."

"He doesn't have as nasty a mind as yours."

"True," McKeever said. "And he doesn't have a nasty ulterior motive."

"Do you?"

"Maybe. Maybe I'm still in love with you. Maybe I want to discredit your boyfriend."

She was staring at him.

He laughed. "I'm just pointing out all the possibilities. Think about them all."

She seemed to be thinking for a long moment, then shook her head rapidly. "Are you planning to follow me to Moscow?" she asked.

He laughed again. "Now think about *that*. How eager do you think they'd be to let me into Moscow?"

"Then you're staying in Paris."

He nodded.

"Where?"

"At the Hotel de Nice. Overnight. Why? Do you want to stay with me?" He wished he hadn't said that; even more, he wished he hadn't wished it. Though it didn't exactly surprise him that he did.

She met his eyes for another long moment. Suddenly she wanted more than anything else just to tell him the truth. She wanted him to hold her. She wanted it to be six years ago, and she wanted to get up from this table and go back to his apartment, and back to who she'd been, and back to what they'd had. But it was all long gone, and much too late. And the man who now sat across the table from her was teasing her, playing with her, working at his job. And his job had something to do with hurting David.

She sighed suddenly. "The reason I asked where you'd be is that I'd like to call you from Moscow tomorrow. I'll tell you everything you want to know,

Luke, I promise you that. But not till tomorrow."
She bit her lip. "I haven't lied to you, Luke; I just
haven't told you everything I know. But I will. Tomorrow. Just give me till then. Trust me till then.
I'll be staying at the Metropole Hotel in Moscow."

"Yes."

"You knew that?"

"Yes."

"Will you trust me?"

He nodded. He already knew everything she
knew; he'd found it in the vault. "Sure. I'll trust
you, I just don't trust your boyfriend." He hesitated.
"Do you?"

She hesitated. "Yes."

He nodded. "Finish your coffee. I'll take you to
the Rodin Museum."

"Good." She smiled. "I've never been to the Rodin Museum."

"I know."

She looked at him. "Do you know everything?"

He laughed. "Not by a long shot," he said.

10.

The Concorde sat on the runway, glinting in the sun. Around it, a ring of armed troops stood at attention. On his way through the terminal building at De Gaulle, Palmer had spotted a half-dozen men with the telltale bulges of holsters in their armpits and the icy, vigilant look in their eyes that spelled out "agent."

Standing on the glass-enclosed moving ramp that had brought them up to the departure level, he'd muttered to Kleber, "Great day to pull a bank job in Paris."

"Huh?"

"Every cop and agent is *here*."

"Oh." Kleber's camera was mounted on his shoulder like a rifle, and he continued to shoot.

Now he was filming the Concorde on the field, with its ring of guards.

"You can see," said the head of airport security,

"that the plane is well-protected. It's been under guard ever since it landed."

"I hope so," Palmer said, and Kleber swiveled, training his camera on the head of security—Monsieur Preterlain, a wiry man in his early fifties—while Palmer held the microphone.

"And what other precautions have been taken," Palmer asked, "to assure the safety of the flight to Moscow?"

"Of the flight itself?" Preterlain asked. "That is not my department. I know the French Air Force is kept on alert and the skies will be watched with special attention. But aside from that, I only know what's been done on the ground."

"And that is?"

"Everything. The plane has been under constant guard. The slight damage done to it yesterday was repaired by regular authorized crews. The plane has been thoroughly checked for bombs and other possible forms of sabotage. The airport is being watched closely. Anyone who looks suspicious will be stopped. Nothing will happen before you take off."

"And after that?"

The Frenchman made a wry, sour expression. "It is the wish of Mr. Sande that the plane take off. He does not wish to be intimidated by terrorists. I agree with that. We have been busy rounding up suspects all through the night. But I cannot know what is happening in Austria, or Germany, or the other countries over which you will be flying."

"But you guarantee there won't be any trouble in France?"

"Monsieur—" the Frenchman rolled his eyes to the sky— "there are no guarantees at all in this world. Terrorism is guerilla war, and, as you Americans know very well, a guerilla war is the hardest to fight. I can only guarantee we have done our best."

Preterlain smiled. "You still don't look very happy, Monsieur. Let me add this: I, myself, would feel safe in taking this flight. Does that make you feel better?"

"Are you taking the flight?"

"But no, Monsieur."

"Then I don't feel better." Palmer laughed. In truth he felt fine. If lightning had broken all the rules and struck twice, there was just no way it could strike them again.

Maggie looked around the departure terminal. It looked, she thought, like the set for a science fiction movie—the airport of the future, with its rising, curving, intersecting ramps, like glass-covered, vertical, cloverleaf highways. McKeever was also glancing around, with that easy, idle look in his eyes. He was standing behind her on the carpeted ramp. She looked at him over her shoulder and smiled. It had been a wonderful Paris afternoon.

"You're still worried?" she asked.

"Who, me?" he said, his gray eyes fixed on the crowds below. "About what?"

"About the safety of the Concorde."

"Oh." He looked at her now and nodded. "You know the French saying—'jamais deux sans trois.' "

"It never rains but it pours."

"That's the loose translation. I mean the tight one."

"Never two without three. Bad things happen in threes."

"Forget it," he said. "It's a dumb superstition. And they'll have enough Air Force fighters in the sky to protect you from anything." They stepped off the ramp. "And I wish you'd take the train."

"The Orient Express?" she laughed.

"Maggie—" He stood in front of her. "It's not the

222

Concorde I'm worried about, it's you. I don't think you're out of danger."

"And I don't think I was ever in it. Except," she conceded, "for that one night when Parker was killed. You're wrong about David. And you'll see that—tomorrow."

He sighed and shrugged. "You're at gate twenty-eight." He pointed. "It's that way."

They started walking.

She said, "I'd like to stop at the duty-free shop."

"It's for suckers," he said. "You can buy almost everything cheaper in town."

"But I didn't," she said.

They took the escalator up one flight, then turned right to the crowded, brightly lit corridor of shops: perfume, liquor, handbags, ties, scarves, china, glassware, shirts, and crowds of shoppers.

Among them she noticed Jean Beauregard, a man who used to work with McKeever in Paris. He looked right through her as though they'd never met. He didn't seem to recognize McKeever either. He had a scarf around his neck and he unwound it quickly as he looked at some ties.

Maggie felt McKeever's hand on her elbow. "I think we ought to buy a tie for Uncle Sam," he said to her, and Maggie frowned, then nodded.

The PA system suddenly announced, *"Air France flight number one-twenty-one now boarding for Rome . . ."*

A salesgirl approached. "Madame?"

"Je voudrais une cravate," Maggie said. She looked at McKeever, but McKeever was looking at a tall blond man who was walking away from the perfume counter. McKeever said, "Wait here," and started to move. Jean Beauregard said to her quickly, "Pardon me, Madam. It's none of my business, but—" he pointed at the counter— "there are no good buys here."

She looked at him, frowning. And again, she understood. He'd simply delivered a message in a pun: *there are no goodbyes here*.

McKeever was gone.

The blond man flashed his identification: De Winter. CIA.

"What's up?" McKeever asked.

De Winter had his eyes on a dark-haired man who was walking ahead of them. "Don't know," De Winter said. "That guy in the blue suit. He checked in for Rome. I don't like him, that's all."

McKeever nodded. Robelle had a man who was leaving for Rome. And De Winter had a hunch.

They were approaching a guarded escalator with a sign above it: PASSENGERS ONLY BEYOND THIS POINT. The man in the blue suit stopped in front of the metal detector and showed a ticket and passport. He put his flight bag and coat on the conveyor that would shuttle it in through the X-ray machine. He started to walk through the metal detector.

Bells didn't ring.

He wasn't armed. But then, he wouldn't be. Not unless he was stupid. He picked up his flight bag and stepped on the ramp that would take him upstairs to gate forty-one, where the PA announced that the flight to Rome was now boarding.

De Winter nodded at one of the guards, jerked his thumb at McKeever, and nodded again.

The two of them passed through the metal detector.

Bells didn't ring.

Both men were armed, but the guard had turned the detector off.

McKeever stepped on the escalator, ten feet behind the blue-suited man. He and De Winter were halfway to the top when one of the guards below yelled, "Monsieur?" and McKeever turned.

The man ahead of him had also turned, looked at the guard, and then started to run.

McKeever and De Winter, their guns in their hands, went after him now. Security guards started closing in, but the dark-haired man dove into a crowd, making it all but impossible to shoot. The man kept running, dropping his flight bag, elbowing passengers. Frightened at the sight of the guns, a few of them screamed; the rest just scattered. The man raced on, and plowed through a waiting room. Guards fanned out, surrounding him now. McKeever and De Winter moved through the crowd, yelling, "Stay back!" But the man moved on, heading for a closed emergency exit, setting off bells. McKeever followed, almost tackled the man, as volleys of shots were fired from behind. McKeever was hit. He stumbled, cursing, and the man got away and started running down the field, pursued by the guards now, passing a plane unloading at a ramp.

De Winter ran up to McKeever. "Okay?"

McKeever looked up at him. "Never been better." Blood was starting to soak through his jeans, but the bullet had only grazed him on the shin.

"I'm afraid," De Winter said, "that that was my bullet."

"Yeah? You got lousy aim," McKeever said. "Go on. You can run a lot faster than I can."

De Winter took off. A counter-terror agent of the CIA, with lousy aim. McKeever started walking, watching the action that was now going on a hundred feet ahead.

The dark-haired man was racing down a runway; an army pursued him—guards, emergency vehicles, trucks. But they didn't get him.

What got him was a plane: a Beechcraft, coming in for a landing. McKeever watched as the plane

225

tried to veer, but its wingtip batted the man in the shoulder, knocking him backward, slicing his chest. He must have had his blood money stuffed in his shirt, because blood-soaked bills went flying through the air.

By the time McKeever got there, the man was dead, buried in money.

De Winter was standing over the body, examining a wallet. "His name's Froehlich. Carl Froehlich."

"Mean anything?" McKeever said.

De Winter shook his head. "Not to me. His face doesn't mean anything either. I just didn't like him. It was only a hunch."

McKeever sighed. If Carl Froehlich was Robelle's man, and he probably was, he'd never get to tell them what his mission had been, what job he'd completed to earn all that money.

The answer would have to come from Robelle.

11.

In the crew room, Metrand and Patroni checked their mail and looked at the dozen-odd company bulletins—special instructions applying to the flight from Paris to Moscow, amendments to be added to their flight manuals.

Special precautions were being taken by the French. The Air Force was on standby; the Concorde flight would be carefully monitored.

"I wouldn't mind a few antiaircraft guns," Patroni muttered. "Or a couple of missiles."

Metrand looked up. "You really think we'll have trouble?"

"No," Patroni said. "But I wouldn't mind a few antiaircraft guns and a couple of missiles, just for good luck, you know what I mean?"

"How about a St. Christopher medal?" O'Neill said behind them. He was grinning.

"Yeah? What's with you?" Patroni muttered. "You look as happy as a clam."

"As an escargot," O'Neill corrected. "Or, to be more exact, a dozen escargot, smothered in butter, drenched in garlic, and followed by a giant plate of roast pork, with a soupbowl of chocolate mousse to finish it off."

"You went off your diet," Patroni concluded.

Metrand shook his head, and gestured with his thumb at O'Neill. "The only man in the world who can cheat on his wife by making love to a menu."

"Well, what the hell," O'Neill said blithely, and Metrand tried to read the expression on his face. Metrand thought again of LeBec's "vision" and hoped O'Neill had forgotten it by now. Metrand believed in neither visions nor omens, but flying with a spooked crew was a curse. A man who thought he saw Destiny coming would not act as quickly as a man who only saw an enemy plane. It was difficult to fly in the face of Fate.

But O'Neill looked fine, cheerful, in control, and it didn't look to Metrand like a bluff.

Patroni filled out the final flight plan. Patroni was officially captain of the run, and Metrand would function as first officer and also take a supervisory role.

Patroni looked up. *"Allons, enfants,"* he said in terrible French.

"What did he say?" O'Neill asked Metrand.

"He said, 'Let's go, kiddies.'"

They walked to the plane.

"Attention, please. This will be your only boarding call for Federation World Airlines flight one-seventeen for Moscow. The Concorde is boarding at gate twenty-eight."

Maggie looked around. There were armed security guards all over the boarding lounge, but no sign of McKeever. Palmer and Kleber were standing by the windows. They were locked in what seemed to be an urgent conversation.

"Can girls listen in?" she asked as she approached.

Palmer looked up. There was strain and excitement showing in his eyes.

"We got the damnedest piece of footage," Kleber said quickly.

"Yeah. But we don't know what it means," Palmer added. "The cops threw a lot of fast French at us. I think the translation was 'none of your business,' and then they almost tried to confiscate the film."

"Did they?"

"No. We've still got it."

"What happened?" Maggie asked.

"We'll tell you on the plane." Kleber grabbed her arm. "I want to get on board before the cops change their minds."

Frowning, Maggie looked over at Palmer, but Palmer was busy looking to his right.

He spotted Tatyana. She was walking, without a trace of a limp, next to Nelli, who seemed to have her eyes on Gregori and Gregori's daughter. And Nelli was wearing lipstick and a dress. Palmer grinned and moved up to Tatyana.

"Well . . . did you have a pleasant evening?"

She smiled at him. "No," she said softly.

He frowned. "No?"

"I love you," she said. "It was a beautiful evening. But also painful."

"Your ankle," he said.

"My heart."

"I see." There were ten people in the line in front of them, waiting to board flight 117. "You can still change your mind," Palmer whispered. "All we have to do is turn around and leave, and take a cab to the American embassy. But once we're on board, there's no turning back. We'll land in Moscow and that's the end of us."

For an answer, she lowered her eyes, then moved up with the rest of the line.

Ahead of them, Maggie entered the plane, and Kleber was showing his boarding pass to the same pretty, dark-haired stewardess who'd flown with them before on the way to Paris.

She didn't look happy. Her smile seemed false.

IV

She furrowed her brow. "Why did Parker have it?"

"How the hell do I know?" he snapped at her.

1.

"What we've got," Kleber said as he settled in the aisle seat next to Maggie, "is a wild piece of film. A gun battle in a boarding lounge, followed by the greatest chase scene since *The French Connection*, followed by a guy getting clipped by an incoming plane." Kleber shook his head. "I don't know who he was—whether he was a terrorist or what, but he had about two dozen cops on his tail, and this one guy, this redheaded cop, made a tackle like Dallas should've done in the Super Bowl. Man! What a—"

"Redhead?" Maggie said. "Was he wearing a uniform?"

"No. Plain clothes."

"A trenchcoat?" She described what McKeever was wearing. "Jeans and a gray turtleneck—"

"Christ, I don't know. Yeah. Maybe jeans. Anyway, he got shot."

She couldn't breathe for a moment.

"Hey," Kleber said, "don't take it so hard. A French cop—"

"Was he—was he all right?"

"I don't know. He fell. I saw blood. And then we ran past him. And the cops got onto us and carted us away. I didn't see him again. He was gone when we got back."

"So he could have walked away."

"Or been carried away. What difference does it make? I mean, a French cop—"

"Are you sure he was French?"

"He was yelling in French."

Which McKeever would have done.

"Hey, look," Kleber said, "the point is—"

But she couldn't listen to his point. She had to know about McKeever. She got up from her seat. The dark-haired stewardess was standing in the aisle. "Please sit down. The plane is in motion."

Maggie looked around; she looked at the runway rushing past the window. It was too late now. She'd have to wait till they got to Moscow to learn what had happened.

"You okay?" Kleber asked.

She nodded dumbly.

Celeste brought two cups of coffee to the flight deck.

"You forgot mine," O'Neill said. "Make it big and black."

Celeste handed a cup to Metrand. She avoided his eyes.

"Bonjour," he said.

She nodded, handing a cup to Patroni, who simply said, "Thanks," and continued checking the instrument panel.

"Hey," Metrand said. "I want to talk to you."

She turned again, eyeing him warily. "What?"

He shrugged. "I think I said a few things last night— I, uh—I was very tired."

She regarded him coolly. "I didn't believe you anyway."

"Hey." He grinned, shaking his head. "I'm not tired now . . . and I still mean them."

She stared at him.

"Believe me," he said. "Let yourself believe me."

She was still staring.

"Hey, Celeste," O'Neill said. "What does a man have to do to get a cup of coffee around here?"

Patroni shot him a quick look.

Celeste flushed.

"I didn't say anything," Patroni said quickly. "I didn't say anything."

"Nobody said anything," Metrand added. "Except me. I just said I love you."

Celeste started laughing. She was still laughing when she walked through the door and back to the cabin, and Metrand felt happy, very deeply happy.

He checked the clock on the control panel. They'd been in the air about twenty minutes. Below them were the vineyards of Burgundy.

Patroni made a small adjustment to the autopilot, and Metrand automatically scanned the instruments, then looked slowly at Patroni's face. "*You're* very quiet," he said.

Patroni shrugged. "Other peoples' happiness makes me quiet. I was thinking about my wife."

Metrand nodded. "I know what that's like. At least you have the honesty to let yourself feel lonely."

Patroni looked at him.

"Listen—" Metrand suddenly grinned— "I know this great woman who works for the French embassy in Moscow—"

Patroni laughed.

The radio cut in with the news that a storm front

was moving through Germany. The Concorde was advised to take a southerly route.

"Ladies and gentlemen, messieurs et mesdames —and comrades." The French captain's voice sounded cheerful. "Because of weather conditions, we'll be changing our course and flying over the Austrian Alps. This will add only a few minutes to our estimated arrival time in Moscow."

Maggie was staring out the window. There was nothing out there but clouds. You couldn't see where you were going or where you'd come from. *An apt analogy,* she suddenly thought. It was bad enough that she didn't know where she was going, that her future seemed thoroughly uncharted now, but what seemed even worse was the fact that she didn't even know where she'd been—that her past had been based on a false premise, a series of bad judgments, that she'd been living in a world that was very different from the one she'd seen—or chosen to see. And now she was in limbo, someplace between the unknown future and the unknown past.

She was only certain of one thing: she did not love David. And yet, if David did as he'd promised, didn't she owe him her loyalty then? And couldn't she then admire his courage? *Shouldn't* she? But her mind kept returning to McKeever. If McKeever was dead . . . But she couldn't hold it in her mind. She could only think of him this afternoon, walking through the Rodin Museum, looking at the incredible, sensual sculpture, stopping in front of a statue, saying nothing, just slightly increasing the pressure on her hand, making her look, making her *see*. And what she'd seen most clearly was McKeever. And she suddenly wished, almost desperately, that it was his baby she was having, that she could share her child with him, and that her child could inherit his clarity, his strength, his perspective.

She felt a hand on her shoulder.

It was Palmer. He was frowning. "Hey—you all right? You look as though you just lost your best friend."

She nodded. "Maybe twice."

He raised his eyebrows.

"If you ever see me falling in love again, Bobby, do me a favor and pretend I'm a football. Give me a good swift kick."

He smiled ruefully. "I don't know what you're talking about, but I know what you mean." He looked at Tatyana, who was sitting with Nelli.

Kleber walked up the aisle, scowling. He was holding a copy of the *Paris Tribune*. "Did you see this?" he said to Palmer.

"No, why?"

Kleber handed him the paper, and pointed at an item:

AMERICAN REPORTER FATALLY SHOT

Los Angeles. Jeffrey Marks, a Washington newscaster, was shot and killed, gangland style, in a . . .

"Jesus!" Palmer sat down. He handed the paper to Maggie. "Why would anyone . . . ?"

She read it, taking a long, slow breath. And then everything crashed together in her head.

Only she and Parker had known about Jeffrey's connection to the papers: the envelope switch. And no foreign agent, nobody else, no mysterious "they" could have discovered it.

But David could have.

Jeff had interviewed David on Thursday.

And he would have been photographed, entering and leaving Harrison Aircraft, with an envelope

237

from WKRV. A blowup of the photo would have shown the name on the envelope. Yes. Of course. When they realized the papers were missing, they'd have checked the photographs. . . .

> . . . an unidentified witness described the gunman as a tall, blonde, good-looking . . .

The same gunman who'd killed Parker, and tried to kill her.

And after he'd failed, the Harrison drone had attacked the Concorde.

She closed her eyes, remembering the scene at Dulles Airport. David had tenderly kissed her goodbye, and then he'd seen Annabelle handing her the envelope. And then, like a trusting idiot, she'd called him ten minutes later and said, "I've got the papers." And *then* his drone had attacked the Concorde.

It all seemed terribly obvious now.

But what about the second attack on the plane? Had he arranged that too?

Why not? she thought wryly. *If at first you don't succeed . . .*

And McKeever had asked her at lunch today about Reims, Strasbourg—who David knew in France.

Only now did she remember who David knew: Andre Robelle at *Service Générale*—a name she'd seen in the papers from Parker, a name connected to the shipment of arms. Somehow the pieces could be made to fit a conspiracy.

"Gangland style," Kleber was saying. "Jeff? Jesus. It doesn't make sense."

Palmer shook his head. "I don't understand it."

* * *

238

"I don't understand it." Patroni said.

"What?"

"I don't know, Paul. There's something wrong—something's vibrating."

Metrand checked the console. The instruments indictated nothing was wrong. "I don't see any—"

Suddenly the plane dipped.

"Paul?"

It leveled off.

"She nosed," Metrand said. He fingered the wheel, waiting. "It's okay. No problem now."

But the door to the flight deck started to rattle.

So did the rudder in Patroni's hand.

"We'd better run a systems check," Metrand said.

"Altimeter," O'Neill said.

"Set and checked," Patroni responded.

"Airspeed indicator?"

"Checked," Patroni said.

The door snapped open.

Both of them turned. It was Celeste.

"There seems to be something wrong." She was frowning. "There's a whistling, banging sound in the cabin. It seems to be coming from the cargo area."

"The cargo door?" Metrand checked the console. If something was wrong with the cargo door, a warning light would go on. There was no warning light. Metrand checked the switch. It wasn't working. "It worked on our preflight rundown," he said. "I'll go back and check it. And we better turn on the seat belt sign."

O'Neill turned it on.

"Celeste, get everyone into their seats."

She nodded and picked up the interphone. "The Captain has turned on the seat belt sign. Please return to your seats and fasten your seat belts."

Metrand got up, squinted at the console, then walked through the flight deck door with Celeste.

He could hear the whistling, banging sound.

"Is anything wrong, Captain?" somebody asked.

"Probably some baggage loose in the hold. Nothing serious. I'm going back to—"

He never finished the sentence. The whistle-bang turned into a roar, and then an explosion.

Explosive decompression!

A gale wind seemed to rip through the cabin as the door connecting the cabin to the hold catapulted open. A bell went off, oxygen masks tumbled from above, and everything that wasn't nailed to the floor or strapped in a seat started flying through the air—flight bags, handbags, pillows, coats, blankets, drinks, newspapers, coffeepots, internal doors—rushing through the air to the back of the plane and out through the gaping hole in the hold, as though they'd been sucked out by a vacuum cleaner.

The passengers were hit by a dance of objects, and then the force of the suction slowed, replaced by the deafening roar of the engines, the biting blast of the icy wind.

Metrand, holding tightly to Celeste and the back of a chair, commanded, "Get on your oxygen masks! Everybody! Fast!" He and Celeste reached for the masks that had dropped from the ceiling in positions on the aisle. Speed was a matter of life and death. The air that was filling the airplane now was the thin, rarified outside air, and at thirty-seven thousand feet above the ground, a human being breathing that air had about fifteen seconds to breathe. Then unconsciousness would come followed rapidly by irreversible brain damage and, finally, death.

Fortunately, Metrand was only a few steps away from the flight deck, and fortunately he'd stopped to answer a question, moving to the left in front of the front row of passenger seats. It was fortunate because the flight deck door had been ripped from its hinges and shot down the aisle.

240

Now that the full, jarring impact of the blast was over, he started for the deck, feeling the plane roll sharply to the left, then start to dive.

At the controls, Patroni, almost deaf from the painful pressure on his eardrums, struggled to keep the plane in control. The first thing he had to do was slow down, and the next thing he had to do was to dive down to a level where the air could be breathed, before the supplemental oxygen was gone.

There were perils in trying to dive too fast, a damaged aircraft could break apart from the added stress of a rapid dive. But on the other hand, the temperature inside the plane was the same as the temperature outside: minus forty-five degrees centigrade. Killing cold. And cold killed fast. You could freeze to death doing too slow a dive.

He banked to the left, then started to dive, as O'Neill reported, "Mayday. Mayday. Concorde one-one-seven. Explosive decompression. We're diving."

Metrand dropped into his seat.

"No good," Patroni said. "I'm losing control. The computer's out. Control system's going."

"One and two are out," Metrand reported.

"Three's about to go."

"Go to backup systems!"

They were tumbling like a leaf.

Maggie sat there, sucking in oxygen. Her feet were freezing. She'd lost her shoes to the force of the suction; it had pulled them off her feet. It occurred to her, as some kind of cosmic joke, that she was barefoot and pregnant, and about to die.

The noise in the cabin was a roar. Her head was splitting. In a few more minutes, everything would split.

Splat.

And David would have won.

She wouldn't be around to make the phone call from Moscow, to tell Monsieur Ravignol to play the tape. To tell Luke what had happened.

If Luke was alive. . . .

"Backup!" Patroni yanked at the switch. "Come on!" he yelled at it. "Give us some help."

"It's okay. It's responding." The controls were heavy, but they were responding, and they eased as Metrand pulled back on the yoke, and the plane descended more slowly, then leveled. "We're back in control." Metrand checked the instruments. "They're working again. Airspeed one-twenty. Altitude eleven thousand feet."

"From thirty-seven." Patroni whistled. "We should win the Olympic diving medal, right?"

At eleven thousand feet the air was breathable—cold as hell, but not as cold as death.

"Pressure's equalized," Patroni said, and took off his mask.

At the radio console, O'Neill was reporting to Munich Center: "We're level at eleven thousand," he said. "Request information . . ."

Patroni was on the intercom. "Ladies and gentlemen, what happened was—we lost a door in the baggage compartment. That wouldn't have happened under normal conditions; it looks like sabotage. But it looks like the Concorde is hard to beat. We've activated backup systems that are working perfectly. At this time we're in communication with Munich Center for landing instructions. I'd like for the flight attendants to distribute pillows. When we make our landing, place the pillow across your knees and put your head on the pillow." He paused for a moment. "And you can stop worrying," he added quickly. "We're going to make it."

Metrand looked at him, nodded, and jerked his chin at a gauge. "We're losing thrust," he said. The altimeter was unwinding again. Already they'd dropped another five hundred feet.

"We're losing fuel," O'Neill barked. "The jettison pumps are open and I can't shut them off."

"Wonderful," Patroni said. "Wonderful. Somebody really did a job on us. What the hell's going on?"

Metrand got on the radio. "Munich Center from one-one-seven. We have engine problems and our fuel is critical. Please advise nearest airfield."

They continued losing altitude. Ten thousand . . . 9,800 . . .

"We show your position," Munich responded, "forty miles due north of the Alps. Innsbruck is your closest airfield. Stand by. Concorde."

"Ninety-five hundred feet, airspeed two-eighty," Patroni reported.

"How long would it take us to get to Innsbruck at two-eighty airspeed?"

Patroni looked through the map book.

They continued losing altitude.

"Fifteen minutes at least," Patroni said.

"Do we have the fuel to make it?"

"No."

Metrand grunted. "Alps, dead ahead."

"We can't climb," Patroni said. "We've gotta go down. Fast. Maybe there's a snowfield."

Metrand closed his eyes. There was a snowfield. He'd skied here. "Yes." He tried to picture it. "The snow lasts all year on the north side. The downhill ski course is very wide, with a bowl at the bottom." He turned to O'Neill. "Get us a heading for Patsch-erkofel."

* * *

Palmer was holding Tatyana's hand. She was weeping quietly. "We're not going to make it, are we?" she said.

"I love you," he answered.

"I want to marry you," she said.

"I'll hold you to that."

"Just hold me."

He held her. "We'll make it," he said.

He looked at the Alps. The Alps were too near; the plane was too low.

"Marry me now," he said.

"Now?"

"Now. Do you, Tatyana Rogov, take me, Robert Palmer as your lawfully wedded husband? Say 'I do.'"

"I do."

"Do you, Robert Palmer, take Tatyana Rogov as your wife? I do. I now pronounce us man and wife. Kiss the groom."

They kissed, long and hard.

"Concorde, you've been cleared for approach to Patscherkofel. Heading zero-four-seven."

"Roger, Munich."

"They're reporting clear skies with twenty-mile visibility. Winds are heavy, from the north, gusting to thirty-two knots."

"Requesting emergency rescue alert."

"We're already on that, Concorde."

"Thanks, Munich. We'll keep you advised."

"Ever come down on your belly?" Patroni asked.

Metrand shook his head.

"Then it'll be the first time for both of us."

Metrand clicked on the intercom. "Celeste, we'll be trying to land in a couple of minutes. Get the passengers ready."

"I will," she answered.

"And Celeste? I love you."

"I trust you," she said.

It was white outside—the fleecy white of the clouds and the icy white of the snow-covered Alps. Nelli rubbed her arms to keep herself warm. "Patscherkofel," she said. "The 'seventy-six Olympics were held here."

They approached the mountainside. It was wide and steep, and marked with crevasses. It sloped downward, ending in a large, hollow bowl.

Gregori nodded. "We try to land here." He looked at his daughter, beside him in the seat by the window. He smiled. "We land here," he said to her in Russian, forming the words so she could read them with her eyes. He turned to Nelli across the aisle. "With luck," he said, and reached for her hand.

"You're in luck," Munich said. "There's still a twenty-foot base of snow. Hard-packed."

"What's the incline of the hill?" Metrand asked.

"Forty degrees, sloping to twenty-seven."

"We're going for it, Munich. Thanks for everything."

"Good luck, Concorde. *Bis bald.*"

"What does that mean?" Patroni asked.

" 'See you later,' in German."

"I'm glad they think so," Patroni said. He looked at the console. "Altitude eighty-five hundred feet. Airspeed one-eighty."

Snow was swirling from the mountaintops, blowing at the window.

Metrand squinted out. "One hell of a crosswind. Look at her blow."

"Eighty-four hundred feet," Patroni announced.

There were mountains all around them, above

them. The plane hit a pocket of turbulence, and jumped.

Patroni steadied it. "Eighty-three hundred feet. Airspeed one-sixty." Below, he could see a make-shift landing strip, built in the snow. Custom-built. Ski patrolmen had planted flares in a neat double row. It lay ahead of them. All they had to do was get there without crashing into the mountains that stood like walls, surrounding them.

"Eighty-two hundred feet."

A horn went off, screaming through the flight deck.

"Anti-stall warning!" O'Neill was yelling.

"I hear it!" The yoke began to fight Metrand's hand.

They had to go in through a pass, a narrow pass between two craggy peaks.

"Like threading a needle." Patroni held his breath.

Still bucking, they rode through the pass.

O'Neill let his breath out slowly. "My God."

"It's not over yet." Patroni looked below. They were racing toward the short, flare-outlined strip. "We'll get only one chance at this bastard."

"This is it," Metrand said.

And the plane swooped down, rocking in the wind, plunging toward the snow.

"Power off!" Metrand yelled, and yanked at the throttles.

And then they were down, with a shuddering jolt, sliding, skidding through the snow, sledding. Snow covered the visor. Zero visibility. Still sliding. The plane wouldn't stop. It was sliding *up* the mountain-side, passing the runway. It sliced through the snow, slammed through a drift. The force of the snow broke open the visor, and it filled the flight deck.

* * *

The roof had caved in. The passenger cabin was buried in snow.

Gregori, stunned, pushed his way out from under the weight of the hard-packed snow.

Irina!

She was trapped. A huge piece of metal was pinning her down—a section of the roof, about ten feet long. It had trapped his daughter and several others.

Gregori, standing waist-deep in snow, reached for it, pulled at it. It wouldn't budge. He tried again, tried to take a deep breath, take the proper position, tried to pretend it was only a weight, just another weight that had to be lifted. He strained, his body shaking from the effort. It had to weigh well over five hundred pounds. Impossible. *Nothing's impossible,* he told himself. *Nothing.* And slowly, slowly, he got it to move.

Palmer was buried under snow. He started tunneling through it, pitching it away, then he dug for Tatyana, like a man digging for buried treasure.

He pulled her out of the snow. She opened her eyes. "Where are we?" she said.

"Halfway up an Austrian Alp, I think."

"Good," she said.

"Good?"

"We can go back to Paris and get married." She smiled. He kissed her, lifted her. He started to carry her out of the plane, and suddenly realized there was no place to go. The snow was hard-packed against the airplane. It covered the windows; it blocked the doors.

They were trapped.

Maggie came to slowly, and wondered where she was. And then she was aware enough to know where she was. She was pinned under broken seats, under snow. She felt herself starting to black out again.

And then Joe Patroni was standing over her, tossing the seats away, lifting her up.

Metrand was on the radio. "What's going on out there?"

"We're trying to dig you out."

"Out of where?" All he could see was a white wall of snow. But he felt the plane suddenly shift, sliding, and he got his answer: they'd overshot the field; they were halfway up the mountainside.

O'Neill said, "Let's go."

"I think we'd better stay where we are till they get here."

"They may not get here." O'Neill looked worried.

The plane slid again.

"Cover the radio," Metrand said urgently and moved to the cabin, looking for Celeste.

The cabin was nothing but snow-covered wreckage. It was awesome, incongruous. Most of the passengers had dug their way out, or been dug out. He found Celeste. A line of blood was streaking her face from a cut on her temple.

He grabbed her arm, and closed his eyes for a moment in relief at seeing her. There wasn't time to tell her all the things he felt, but he looked in her eyes and knew she knew them, that she felt them too. "What was the boarding count?" he said.

"Forty-three."

He looked around at the cabin, tried to get a count.

"We're all here," she said. "Forty-three. A few broken bones and, I think, one concussion, but we're all here."

"And so are the marines," he said.

A hole had suddenly appeared in the snow; the sun was streaming through the burst-open roof.

A ski patrolman peered through the roof; he dropped down a rope ladder.

Passengers started to climb up the rope.

2.

The hospital corridor was crowded—a lot of gawkers, a lot of reporters.

McKeever had to flash a lot of identification and a lot of teeth before he got to the right waiting room and the right doctor: a Dr. Kraus, who wore rimless glasses and had a bald head with a narrow border of iron-gray hair.

"Maggie Whelan?" McKeever said. "How is she? Where is she?"

The doctor squinted. "I have seen so many—"

"Blonde, beautiful—she was wearing a pinkish sweater and a—"

"Oh, yes. Mrs. Whelan. Yes. A lot of bruises, a broken wrist. But otherwise, she's fine." The doctor smiled. "She and the baby are both fine."

McKeever looked up.

"She was very lucky," the doctor went on. "It would be easy to miscarry at this stage of pregnancy, but the tests show she's fine. By the way, it's a boy."

McKeever just nodded. "Where is she?" he asked.

"Room one-twenty-three. She was exhausted, on top of everything else. I wanted her to rest. She can leave, of course, anytime she likes." The doctor studied McKeever. "Are you her husband?"

"Yes," McKeever replied.

When she saw him, she closed her eyes and started to cry.

"That's a fine greeting," he said as he sat on the bed.

She reached for his hand, and suddenly her face was buried in his chest. He stroked her hair.

"Hey," he said, "it's all right. You're all right."

"I thought you were dead," she said. "I heard—"

"You thought *I* was dead? That's a switch. How—?"

"At the airport. You were shot."

He nodded.

"What happened?"

"I'll tell you later. It's unimportant."

She was crying again.

"Hey, Maggie, Maggie." He cupped her chin, lifted her face, kissed her slowly. After a while, he pulled back and smiled. "That felt like a two-week vacation in the sun."

"Would you like to go for a month?" she asked. "We have a package tour. . . ."

He shook his head slowly.

She closed her eyes and leaned back on the pillows. "I don't blame you," she said. "I'm a nice place to visit, but you wouldn't want to live here."

He raised his eyebrows. "I wouldn't want to live there for only a month. I'm a greedy bastard. I'd want forever."

She looked at him. "Oh, Luke. Oh, Luke. So

251

would I." She lowered her eyes. "But it isn't that simple. I have to tell you . . . I'm having—"

"My baby."

She looked up.

He shrugged. "About six years overdue," he said. "That's the longest gestation period of any living mammal. I bet the kid'll come out on roller skates."

"You knew?"

He shook his head. "I don't know what you're talking about. Why don't you try and get some sleep?"

"Because I've got a lot to tell you. Luke—in a vault—"

"Relax," he said. "We got them. Your friend made a phone call to his partner in Paris, and told him where the papers were. We bugged the phone call and got them first."

"Oh. What—?"

"Are you sure you want to hear all this now?"

"Do you think I could sleep without hearing it? I've been stupid, Luke. At least let me go to sleep smart."

"Hey, listen. You haven't been stupid. You've just been—" he thought it over—"stupid."

She laughed. "I love you."

"That's what I mean. Stupid," he said. "All right. Here's your story. Harrison and Robelle were in business together. Parker got the proof of it, along with the blueprints—"

"Blueprints of what?"

"Of a SCAM. He's got a sense of humor, your friend."

"He isn't my friend."

"I know."

"What's a SCAM?"

"A counterfeit SAM."

"What?"

"A SAM is a—"

"Soviet missile."

"Right. And Harrison was building counterfeit SAMs. He was selling them to anyone who wanted to buy. And when the missiles were used—like the one in Iran—it would look like the Russians had been the suppliers. That's about as dangerous a game as you can play."

"I don't understand."

"He was covering himself. No one could trace the missiles to an American manufacturer. It's a damn good way to start World War Three."

"I don't follow."

"Set a bunch of those off in Saudi Arabia, and it's not unlikely, because that's where the next revolution may be brewing. Now it looks like the Russians are making a bid for a left-wing coup, arming a revolution."

"My God!"

"Yeah."

"You mentioned Iran. *Was* that his missile?"

McKeever shrugged. "I don't have all the answers, Maggie. It could have been. But he's out of business now."

"What—what's happening to him?"

"I imagine that, just about now, he's being arrested. We got Cooper—that was your friendly neighborhood gunman. He—maybe you can fill *me* in here—Jeffrey Marks, he was—"

"I read it." She sighed, then explained about the envelope switch and her eyes misted again. "Poor Jeffrey. He didn't even know what it was all about. Oh, Luke. It's all so senseless."

"It made sense to them."

"There's somebody else who might be in danger: Annabelle—"

"Nobody else is in danger," he interrupted. "It's all over, Maggie. The head of security at Harrison—who is not the greatest genius you'd ever hope to meet—" McKeever shrugged. "But I guess he doped at least part of it out. Anyway, he put your production assistant in protective custody. But there's nobody left to protect her from now." He paused. "Halpern hung himself."

Maggie winced.

"We've got Robelle. He talked to save his neck. All we've got to do is wrap it up now and tie it with a ribbon."

"Isn't it over?"

"I have to go to Strasbourg."

She looked at him, frowning. "What's in Strasbourg?"

He grinned. "A poker game," he said. "A movie I want to see. A gorgeous brunette."

"In other words, don't ask."

"In other words, don't ask. I'll tell you tomorrow."

"I'll be in Russia tomorrow."

He looked at her. "The doctor said it's okay?"

She nodded. "The doctor said it's okay."

He nodded slowly, rubbing his jaw. "We're gonna have one hell of a marriage," he said. "Somebody always flying off someplace . . ."

"Well—" She smiled. "Look at the bright side. If one of us is always flying off someplace . . ."

"Yeah?"

"We can always get home a lot faster on the Concorde."

McKeever threw back his head and laughed.

McKeever was gone.

The blind man flashed his identification: Dr. Wigten